Diane Maender was born in Salt Lake City but soon thereafter life and work and love set her adrift. She has lived in Port of Spain, Houston, Boston, Washington, D.C., Vienna, Dubai, Key Largo, and Cairo, each place leaving an indelible mark on her mind and heart. She currently lives in Cairo with her husband and three children. This is her first book for children.

For Colton, Tyler, Lila—and all those who choose adventure.

Diane Maender

DEAR MAISIE, I'M SORRY

AUSTIN MACAULEY PUBLISHERS™

LONDON • CAMBRIDGE • NEW YORK • SHARJAH

A CIP catalogue record for this title is available from the British Library.

ISBN 9781398417311 (Paperback)
ISBN 9781398417342 (ePub e-book)

www.austinmacauley.com

First Published 2022
Austin Macauley Publishers Ltd®
1 Canada Square
Canary Wharf
London
E14 5AA

Above all, thanks to Corey, my first reader and partner-in-adventure.

It's me. Nora.

No—don't stop reading.

Please.

The lies corrupted me!

No, that's not quite right. I corrupted the lies. Your twisted, dark, beautiful lies…

Maisie, what I'm saying is this: please let me try to make you understand. Let me try to explain why I did all the terrible things I did.

Part One
Into the Desert

Chapter 1

Someone Is Lying to You

Maisie, it all started on a Tuesday morning. Last August.

My dad and not-really-mother sat across from me at the breakfast table. They held hands and stared at me with their four lying eyes, which were as wet and glassy as a pond.

The cuckoo clock ticked. The linoleum floors glistened. The air outside shimmered.

Because, Maisie, there—just outside our window—was one of the fiercest deserts on earth.

I picked up the photo in front of me. A woman sat cross-legged on the ground, drinking from a tiny cup. The woman's curly hair was wild, uncombed. A scarf embroidered with skulls draped loosely around her neck. A tattoo of an olive-green dragon snaked from her spidery wrist, up past her elbow.

Bless her heart.

"So this is my mom," I said.

My not-really-mother pursed her lips and nodded. With new eyes, I took in her Pepto Bismol pink lipstick, her glossy blonde hair. Truth be told, we're nothing alike.

Also, her name is Candy.

"Where is she now?" I asked.

The shamal winds—which race across the big dunes of the empty quarter to here, on the edge of the Arabian Gulf—battered our windows with sand.

Candy and Dad looked at one another. Candy nodded. Dad pulled a notebook card from the pocket of his shirt, then discarded the card onto the table.

"Well, hell, darling. We don't know. Truth is, she took off shortly after you joined us here on earth."

He glanced up to gauge my reaction. I stared back at him with what I hoped were eyes as ice-cold as I felt.

Our framed family photo rattled against the wallpaper and tilted off-kilter.

"I know it's not what you had hoped to hear. But it's the truth. She disappeared right into thin air. We haven't heard from her since then. Could be six feet underground for all we know. That's why we waited to bring this up to you. It seemed an unnecessary cruelty, if you asked me."

Hiccup.

Maisie, I think we can agree that Dad rarely blossoms under duress.

I placed the photo down and picked up my favorite necklace. I turned it over in my palm, considering it like I never had before.

I had been told over the years that my necklace was a christening gift from Grandmamma. How ridiculous, you must think. What kind of Acadian grandma gives an antique elephant necklace to a baby?

But I don't have to tell you that Grandmamma is an odd woman. An odd woman whose home—and all its alligator art, molasses-thick air and gnarled wild oaks—roots me firmly into place.

The lie fit, Maisie. I cannot dispute the fact.

But it was a lie nevertheless.

I threw the necklace back onto the table. It landed with a thud.

Candy grabbed my hand with hers. Her pointy nails pressed into my wrist.

"Honey, when I met your father, you were just this adorable little thing, all fat rolls and red cheeks…and, Lord knows, I was simply born to be a mother." She paused for a moment, apparently lost in the memory. "What I'm trying to say is that you were wanted."

The last word hung in the air. I hadn't even thought to question that yet.

"But you lied. About everything," I said, stating the obvious fact before us. I was stunned, yes, but something else coursed through me, deeper. Something that felt a little like stepping barefoot onto the sizzling sand outside.

A single bead of sweat rolled down from Dad's receding hairline, across his cheek, and then became wedged in his mustache. Hiccup.

Candy's nails pulsed into my wrist as she squeezed my hand—a gesture that, I think, was supposed to be a sort of hand-hug.

"Things are not always black and white, honey," Candy continued after seeing that Dad was unable to say anything. "Someday, when you're a mother, you'll understand. I promise."

"But you're not really a mother, are you?"

I was just thinking out loud, but my words sliced her through clean. She drew in a sharp breath, released my hand

and stood. With one quick move, she straightened our family portrait.

Candy never could tolerate anything helter-skelter.

Heat blossomed across my chest, then crawled up to my neck and finally to my face.

Maisie, I regret saying what I did.

Hiccup.

Candy said nothing as she spooned coffee grounds into the coffee maker. Her back was turned but the sound of a single sniffle gave her away.

I stood up and walked over.

"Sorry, Mom. I'm just a little confused, it's all."

Candy pulled me into a tight side-hug. My shoulder painfully jabbed into her bony sternum. Above me, she dabbed her runny mascara with a single balled-up piece of tissue.

"I know, honey. I know."

"There's one more thing," Dad interrupted. He was ruddy, but his faculty of speech had returned at last. "Nora, you're growing up fast. I say it's high time we treated you like the young woman you are."

Hiccup.

Lord.

"It's about my vocation. My life's work, so to speak." Candy placed a bagel in front of him. Dad took an enormous bite. A glob of cream cheese became stuck in his mustache and wagged at me as he chewed. He washed it down with a gulp of coffee. A dribble ran down his tie and onto his shirt, puddling where his shirt gaped between the buttons.

"The bottom line is…" Hiccup. "… I'm a spy."

When I said nothing, Candy clarified: "CIA, honey. Know it?"

Chapter 2

A Coincidence Is Never Just a Coincidence

Maisie, let me back up. I fear I've rushed ahead without thinking things through. As I tend to do.

Dad and Candy did not choose to tell me the truth out of the goodness of their hearts.

No.

Lord, no.

This story begins one day earlier. Monday. When our moving crates still sat in their packaging. When the grocery store sat undiscovered three and one-quarter blocks away. And, when I—the venerable Nora Penderling—was still thirteen years old and an idiot.

Dad craned his neck as he eased our 1990 Hyundai Odyssey spy-mobile out of the driveway.

"The souk..." he said, rearranging his paunch. "...has always been the beating heart of this merchant town. Its veritable soul. It's the very first thing we should see."

Dad paused to wave at Candy, who was unpacking boxes in the kitchen. Her smile was just a pinch too cheerful.

"Please pick-up milk. MILK," she mouthed through the window.

Cars raced by us on both sides as we cruised onto the entrance ramp of the seven-lane highway at a speed that was far, far too slow. Dad stole a glance down at the directions Candy had written out for him in her tall, slanted cursive. A horn blared as he nearly smashed into the car in the next lane. Circles of sweat blossomed under the armpits of his lavender linen shirt.

Driving has never been Dad's strong suit.

Thankfully, the traffic soon slowed the pace around us to non-life-threatening speed. Dad prattled on as we lurched forward. But I tuned him out. I pressed my forehead against the window to stare at my strange new home.

Piles of sand, construction cranes and wilted trees whipped by, all of it—even the very sky itself—covered with dust. A construction worker, shoulders slumped, looked up and locked eyes with me through the window.

I shifted in my seat, suddenly aware of AC-cold leather seats sticking to my pale thighs.

At last, we arrived in old Dubai. Paint peeled off nearly every tan wall of every tan building, revealing even more layers of tan. The few people outside shielded their heads with scarves and umbrellas, leaning forward towards their destination as if walking through a blizzard.

I had never in my life experienced the kind of heat that required outerwear. I made a mental note to tell Grandmamma. She would tilt her head back and laugh.

"Lorrrr', have mercy…" she would say.

Maisie, you should know that unlike everyone else who graces this earth, Grandmamma never gets tired of my stories.

Every summer she plies me with pralines, leans back in her rocker and says:

"Now, tell me everything. Take me there, sugar."

Those are always some fine moments.

Dad parked the car and then we ducked into narrow alleyways of the souk. And, in the long shadows of the tall buildings above, I finally saw some color.

Traders sat in front of tiny shops selling intricately carved lanterns, tiny bottles of perfume, barrels of brilliant red spices and Persian rugs. They wore long, white kandoras, black abayas and colorful saris. A smoky-sweet scent I couldn't yet identify filled the air. I leaned towards a shop, lured, primarily, by the mobile air conditioning unit humming outside.

"Come inside my shop and have a look," said a trader.

"Special deal just for you," said another, sweeping his hand as if to will me into his shop.

Dad struck up a conversation with one of the traders, and I hung by on standby. I hopped from one leg to the next, broadcasting my impatience. Lord knows, there is nothing quite as painful as stasis in the heat.

Dad paused for a moment when he noticed my impatience. Then he waved me off with my new cell and a promise to meet back at the car in an hour.

"Remember, Nora…" he said as I shuffled away.

"Yes, Dad?"

"First thing in an emergency?"

"Get off the X. Got it."

We Penderlings are always prepared.

At first, I wandered aimlessly down the alleyways. I picked up tiny camels and treasure boxes, genie lamps and embroidered pillows. I scuttled away when anyone approached to encourage a sale. But, after only a few minutes, all the shops and all the shopkeepers started to blend together into an Arabian kaleidoscope of claptrap, balderdash, riffraff.

Was I lost? I should turn around...

But, at the very end of a narrow alleyway, something caught my eye and drew me to it: a tidy line of tiny elephants, carved of teak. Without thinking, my hand found its way to my necklace. I had always loved elephants (Or so I had been told).

Unlike every other shop I had passed, there was no eager merchant outside, but something about the store beckoned me inside anyways. And I couldn't resist its pull.

The inside of the shop was dim, empty. A single, unlit light bulb hung from the ceiling by a chain. An old clock ticked. Light filtered in sideways through the windows caked with dust.

Was the shop even open?

I couldn't leave. Not yet. I was busy gaping.

Elephants covered every inch of the shop's walls and shelves: elaborate elephant masks, vibrant batiks, even an old, wooden clock carved into the shape of an elephant, an elaborate headdress hanging low over her big, sad eyes.

I had never seen this many elephants in one place before—and all so unique! Each elephant was a work of art, a feast for my elephant-loving eyes...

"Miss has been here before?"

I flinched.

A tiny woman interrupted my reverie. She was so close that I could feel her hot breath on my cheek. No, on my neck. She was at least a head shorter than me. From my perch above,

I could see flecks of grey in her dark hair, pulled tightly back into a bun.

"No, never," I said, taking a teensy step backward. "But I'm glad I found your store. So many beautiful elephants…" I turned my eyes back to the walls, hoping she, too, would politely peel hers away from my neck.

But her eyes didn't peel. Not an inch. And her dark brows were up—way up—turning her forehead into a series of notebook lines.

The door opened briefly, letting in the sounds of the chaotic souk outside. It slammed shut again. Silence.

"May I?" she said, turning her palm up, eyes still locked on my necklace.

How could I refuse? I unclasped the necklace and handed it to her.

She turned it over in her palm. "I never thought I'd see this again." She shook her head.

The woman raised her eyes to mine, took me in head to toe.

"So, then. You must be Nora."

Her dark eyes were so close, they flicked right and left at mine, searching for something. She found it. "Yes, just as I thought."

Still clutching my necklace, she turned to walk to the back of the shop and disappeared behind a beaded curtain. The beads swung together, clinking. The air conditioner clicked on. A single bead of sweat raced from the nape of my neck down to the small of my back.

How on earth did this tiny woman know my name?

Chapter 3

There Is No Such Thing
as a Coincidence

Maisie, when presented with something strange, I have found the mind forces the facts to fit. After I was left alone inside the strange elephant shop, possibilities flipped through my head like a shuffling deck of cards: Had Grandmamma, somehow, traveled here and found this exact shop years ago? Had I, somehow, broadcasted my name upon entering? Was there another Nora who happened to have the exact same necklace?

No. No. Not likely.

I couldn't, then, find a reasonable explanation, but I was confident that one existed.

Still, curiosity got the better of me...

I paused to gather my courage, then pushed aside the beads and stepped across the threshold.

I blinked in the bright light. This wasn't another dim room as I had expected, but a courtyard—and a lovely one. An old acacia tree stood in the center. Paper lanterns and white fabric draped from its branches.

The woman stood facing the tree's wide trunk, her back turned and her chin pointed up toward the sky.

"Excuse me, ma'am?" I whispered politely, as I drew near.

She swung around.

"Just wanted to see if I could, possibly, you know, get my necklace back," I said.

She stared in shock at the necklace dangling in her right hand.

"Oh, Miss, forgive me. I didn't mean to take it from you. I forget myself sometimes." Her eyes softened. She handed the necklace back to me.

A turquoise sari embroidered with gold wrapped around one of her shoulders circled around her midsection, then draped down to her ankles. She tilted her head just slightly as she took me in once again.

(She has a habit of doing that, I learned later. But you know this already, Maisie. Because this is Kiyoma, of course.)

The silence lingered, and I realized she expected me to speak. She expected an explanation. Which was crazy, of course, because if anything, I felt that she was the one who owed me an explanation. It was a strange sort of standoff. One in which I had a distinct feeling that I was missing something. Something crucial.

"Why are you here today, Miss Nora? Is your mother here with you?" Kiyoma asked at last. She peered behind me.

"No, she's not here," I said.

"Did she send you?"

I stared at her speechless, confused as to why on earth Candy would send me to this strange place.

"She hasn't told you, then?" Her eyebrows narrowed; her head listed even farther to the right.

I needed to leave. I needed time to weave through the labyrinth of alleyways outside, back to Dad and the car.

"Hasn't told me what?" But I couldn't help myself. (Could you?)

Kiyoma paused. Then she spoke slowly, as if she were choosing each word with care.

"I know that necklace because it was once mine. Before it was stolen from me by your mother. Thirteen years ago."

I couldn't detect a hint of anger in her face. If anything, she smiled ever so slightly.

"Are you sure you didn't know this already, Miss Nora?"

Of course, Maisie, I didn't know the truth about my mother then. Not yet. So, I smiled. This version of facts struck me as so absurd it was fantastic: Candy stealing a necklace?

You should know that Candy always sits in the front row at the church. She uses her right index finger to underline each word in each Bible verse. She makes eye contact with the pastor, even though everyone knows he can see our sins blinking neon just by looking in our eyes.

No, Candy didn't steal the necklace. Of that, I was sure.

As if reading my thoughts, Kiyoma grabbed my hands and looked straight into my eyes. Her grip was firm—surprisingly firm—despite her tiny frame. I leaned back slightly, away from the force of her being. But she moved closer still, her face just inches from mine. She scanned my eyes as if she were decoding a line of hieroglyphics.

"Yes. Fate is an unusual thing…" she started. Still gripping my hands, she tilted her head back to look up through the branches to the yellow sky above.

Lord. How on earth would I escape now?

"…I'm sorry, I need to leave," I interrupted. I would be in serious trouble with Dad if I were late in getting back to the car.

But when Kiyoma's face came back down to earth, she had a priestly smile and eyes that had glossed over like she was in another world entirely.

"Thirteen years ago, your mother sat right here, under this tree. I remember this as if it were just yesterday because she changed my life. She told me all about her path. The lying. The stealing. The coercion." She waved one hand as if pushing away an ugly thought.

My mind churned. I needed to escape.

"But she had to alter the course of her destiny. Because fate had blessed her with a baby girl. She was pregnant with you, Miss Nora."

I leaned back. Kiyoma's grip was tight.

"It wouldn't be easy. Your father said he couldn't…wouldn't…join her in this new life. She would have to do it alone. Raise you, I mean, without…Walter, isn't it?"

She released my hands. I stumbled several steps back.

Walter. When I was finally free to escape, the word nailed me to the spot.

"I think that's what drew her into my shop. My strong female elephants. She wanted to find something special for you. Perhaps, for herself, too. You must understand, fate had dealt me a terrible blow then, too. That was the year of the tsunami back home, and I had lost my house, my family, everything. So I told your mother about this necklace—the only thing of value I had left. I told her that it held a sort of

26

blessing for my family over the generations. Yet, I had to do the impossible. I had to sell it. My baby was sick. I, too, needed a strength I wasn't sure I had."

Her eyes turned dark and bottomless as a black hole as she looked down at her hands.

My mind scrambled to find a plausible explanation, any explanation…

"She left that afternoon. Both of us needed to think things through. But the next morning, my necklace was gone. The only thing of value I had left in the world had been stolen." She turned her dark eyes to me. I flinched, ready for another blow. "I suppose Natalya wasn't done lying and stealing after all…"

Natalya?

The muezzin's call to prayers boomed down from the top of the minaret next door, swept down into the courtyard, and deafened my racing heart. Many thoughts raced through my mind then, but the simplest called me to action: Get off the X.

I backed away, quickly, toward the curtain.

"Wait, Miss Nora, please. I have to tell you the rest."

"…sorry, I have to get back to my dad," I mumbled, as I fled past the beaded curtain and her army of elephants. I pushed open the door.

"Walter?" Her question was the last sound I heard before the door slammed shut, thrusting me out into the anonymous chaos of the souk.

Turns out, Maisie, I wasn't the only one a little behind on the facts of my life.

27

Chapter 4

Always — Pay — Attention

Now, it must be said, Maisie, that all the clues were there that Dad was a spy. They were scattered across my life, like the puzzle pieces spilled across our living room floor.

The endless international moves. The ambiguous nature of Dad's job. The fact that, at just four years old, I knew how to keep my head on a swivel, get off the X…

I remember once—I must have been nine or ten—Dad called me into his home office. He sat behind his huge desk, stroking his mustache, and turning a coin over and over in his palm.

"Darling, I'd like to show you something. A guiding principle for my life, so to speak."

He pushed his chair back, handed me the coin over the desk.

The coin was heavy, fair heavier than it appeared. *Veritas*, it said on one side. Truth.

I inspected it for a long time, turning it over and over to look at both sides of the coin. But I didn't understand. Why was truth a guiding principle for an international marketing consultant? What was he trying to say? And if this was the key perk of the job, well…

I handed it back, nodding like an idiot.

But I should have suspected right then. I should have suspected that it wasn't the *Veritas* that was important. It was the other side of the coin that was important. The un-veritas side that defined our fraud-of-a-life.

Oh, Maisie, it all seems so obvious now, doesn't it? But it's so terribly hard to find something you're not looking for...

Well. For now, we fast-forward two days—two days past when Dad and Candy admitted the truth over breakfast. It was Thursday, the first day of school. I was standing before the closed door of my parent's bedroom. My fist froze in the air just before it knocked on the door.

Because, from behind the door, Candy hissed, "What kind of mother abandons her own child?"

I paused, considering. Then, I replaced my fist with my ear and pressed it to the wood.

This was the only way to find out more, I consoled my poor, unblemished soul. During the last two days, Dad and Candy had met my many questions about Natalya with uncomfortable silence.

"It's not all that simple. You, of all people, should get that." Dad said. His voice was as flat as a frying pan.

"Well, one thing's for sure. Nora's too young to know all the lurid details about Natalya. And you, frankly," Candy said. "She's only 13!"

"Nora has a right to know about her birth mother. You know it." Dad's voice inched closer to the door where my ear was superglued.

"Her family is right here! You and me. We're the ones who've raised her. Fed her. Loved her. That's what matters."

Candy's voice turned low and slow, roasting Dad on a spit. "And what if she talks about all this at school? What will people think of you? Of me! Goodness' sakes. This whole thing is absurd, Walter. We cannot allow it."

The door swung open, depositing me face-first into the room. I stumbled but recovered. So did Candy. She plastered a weird grin on her face.

"Oh, sweetie, you look darling in that uniform. You excited for your first day?"

Candy glistened, as usual. She walked toward me, arms outstretched, but paused at a distance. "I'd kiss you if I hadn't already put my face on."

According to Candy, first impressions matter.

I pulled at my knee-length navy skort and yanked at my faux tie. A huge navy bow stuck out sideways from my head.

"Dumb Brits," I said.

One thing about me, Maisie: I've always excelled at world history. For example, I know the British are responsible for this and every other ridiculous school uniform I'd endured across the globe.

After breakfast, the three of us pulled out of the driveway.

"Hey, darling, I've been thinking. We've been thinking," Dad said, nodding once over to Candy. "Now that we are all aware of our…situation, I think it's about time we talk about how we Penderlings can better protect ourselves. Improve our collective security, so to speak."

Protect ourselves from what?

"The first and most important rule is Always—Pay—Attention." Dad's voice came out clipped, as if he were imprinting them onto a bumper sticker.

Always Pay Attention!

30

"What's behind us?" he asked.

(He wasn't kidding.)

I craned my neck around. Dad interrupted before I had laid eyes on a thing.

"White Toyota, license plate E23257. Memorize that. Write it down. Whatever makes it stick." He jabbed his finger at me.

I unzipped my backpack to locate a pen.

But the truth is, Maisie, no one pays attention, not really. How often do we float through a day without even noticing who pulled out behind us when we left the driveway in the morning and how that same person was there behind us again, in the afternoon? Because it's too exhausting—always paying attention. And, for the most part, ignorance is bliss. Until it isn't. (That's why this part is important.)

By the time I had a pen and paper in hand, all I could remember was "Toyota."

"Y'all hold on." Dad took a sudden right turn into another quiet neighborhood. The wheels screeched, and I flung sideways. "What's behind us now?"

I swung around. "Nothing?"

"Good. But too obvious. Second Rule…Never. Act. Strange."

I had a few questions about that one, given the source.

Dad slowed the van as we neared an enormous empty lot of sand. I could see my new school bus on the other side. A two-foot curb stood in our way.

Dad yanked the wheel right and accelerated over the curb. The tires spun for a moment, then caught, bouncing us across the sandy lot and kicking up a tornado of dust. I slumped down in my seat as we drew near to the front gate of the school. A neat line of SUVs, children and their parents all gaped as the cloud of dust caught up to the Penderling automobile, then settled over us like a bad omen.

"Rule number three…Never. Be. Predictable."

Turns out, my new school was no different from any other school I'd attended. It was full of bright-eyed teachers from Wisconsin hoping for the great international experience and an army of thirteen-year-olds with nannies.

But, right before dismissal, when our class lined up to march down the stairs and out the door, something important happened. Something worthy of your attention.

The alpha-female in the class, the one who I had observed earlier in the day organizing her locker by color-coded subject, jabbed me in the arm.

"Hey, Curly," she said, "what's with the hair?"

She was tall and spoke loudly and, generally, took up lots of space in the universe. I found my eyes following her every move throughout the day. And I hated them for doing that.

"What about it?" I asked.

"That bow." She spat out the word as if it were a black jellybean.

"Just part of the uniform…" I trailed off. I looked around with new eyes. Not a single person on campus was wearing a bow. How had I missed this until now?

(I would kill Candy later.)

"…I just happen to like bows," I said. I unclipped it from my hair and threw it into my bag.

"Well, you really shouldn't wear it again. It's weird. No offense."

That was it: That was the moment I knew we would be best friends.

To me, true friends shoot straight as an arrow.

"You have a pen mark on your face," I said.

"It's the latest fashion, stupid."

I pointed to her nose. She rubbed it off.

"I'm Nora. New here." I offered my hand for a handshake. She ignored it, busy scanning the crowd as we burst through the doors to the blinding sunshine outside.

"I'm Alexandra. But people call me Al," she shouted over her shoulder as she darted off, then disappeared into the crowd.

Dad waved at me from the back of the eager group of parents. His face looked expectant as I drew closer. I braced myself for questioning.

"License plate number?"

I rolled my eyes.

(That would be E23257, Maisie. Pay attention.)

Chapter 5

Simple Plans Are the Best Plans

You must be desperate for an update. What had I learned about Natalya? How had I leveraged elicitation, surveillance, and coercion to get closer to the truth about my real mother?

Well, Maisie, I was still unaware of the range of options at hand.

After weeks of me begging, Dad had unearthed only one additional photograph of Natalya. To my list of known facts about my real mother (necklace thief, runaway mom), I added only one fact: strange tactical fashion sense.

Dad and Candy stood firm: I was too young for any other details.

Feeling helpless and confused, a thick cloud descended over me. And then September melted into October with no notable change in mood or weather. By noon, the streets could still fry chickens. One day after school, I tried to cut across the sandlot behind our house. A million tiny grains of sand stuck to my leg and burned.

My heart raced when Grandmamma sent a picture of a carved orange pumpkin sitting on her pretty porch.

Lord, Maisie, I ached for home.

And then, finally, something happened. Something that that thrust me out of my gloom and forced me to consider the range of options at hand.

It was Friday. Al and I were at the Polo Club where her family had a membership.

"Curly, your problem is that you're not going with the flow," she said. She kicked her legs, which were dangling in the electric-blue water of the chilled pool.

"What do you mean?" I asked, putting one hand to my brow to shield my eyes from the sun's glare. I probably should have brought some sunglasses.

"You're just not. C'mon." She threw her hands up. "It's a sunny day. We're here at the pool. Order a pumpkin-flavored snow cone if it'll make you feel better."

She had a point. I had been a bit mopey about the ridiculous yellow pumpkins.

Al sat perfectly at ease in her red swimsuit, looking at me through the largest, white sunglasses I'd ever seen. When the silence lingered, she pulled down her sunglasses to mid-nose to look at me over the rims.

"Look, I know you're upset. But trust me when I say that no one really knows their mom. No one." She nodded at nanny Consuela, whose nose was buried in her phone as usual.

I understood what she implied: I had not once met Al's mother in the two months we had become friends.

I looked past the pool to the perfectly manicured polo field beyond. A throng of ex-pats lounged on the hoods of their cars, their hands filled with tiny food on skewers. They whooped and hollered at the action on the field, nearly spilling their bubbly drinks. One fat man teetered sideways and then toppled from the hood to the grass.

A waiter arrived at the poolside.

"Fresh baked chocolate chip cookies, girls?"

"Yes, please," Al said, grabbing one.

I had to admit: going with the flow seemed like fun.

I reached for a cookie, licking my lips.

But, suddenly, a large, dark shape descended and thwacked me in the face.

That's where I blacked out.

When I came to, I was lying flat on my back on the hot pavement. A lifeguard's head was directly over mine, casting a long shadow over my face.

"Miss, you've been attacked. By a crow," he explained, digging into his first aid kit.

My forehead throbbed. My attacker had clawed a series of wide gashes above my right eye as he grasped and lunged for my cookie. By the looks of the crumbs on my chest, he had succeeded.

I turned my head right and left to find Al. The pool area was nearly deserted. She huddled inside, dripping, behind the closed door of the pool house, her warm cookie clasped to her chest like a touchdown football. When our eyes met, she put one hand up. A self-conscious wave, I think.

That's when it hit me, Maisie: I'm just not built to go with the flow. I had to know more about my real mother. I had to know the truth. Whatever the cost.

But how?

The lifeguard cleaned my gashes, then dabbed my forehead with antibiotic cream. I winced from the pain.

36

Consuela, apparently the only one brave enough to stick to my side, flailed her hands like an angry bird.

"Madam will be so angry. Madam will be so angry! Sir, you must turn off the birds," she screeched.

The lifeguard's head moved to the side, and I squeezed my eyes shut in the sun. A long shadow returned, and I opened my eyes again. Al's brows narrowed above me.

"Sorry, Curly," she mumbled. "Sorry I ran away while you almost died." She took a big bite of her cookie and licked her wrist where the chocolate had melted and dripped down.

I nodded. How she could eat at a time like this, Lord only knew.

I gathered my strength, then propped myself up on my elbows to look into her cowardly eyes. One puffy eyelid drooped down low over my right eye, giving me what I hoped was an intimidating pirate stare.

"I need to know more about my real mom. You've got to help me. I hate to state the obvious, but now you owe me."

That evening, Al and I paced back and forth inside her cavernous bedroom, our feet plodding in step across her white-shag rug. A crystal chandelier glimmered high above our heads, reflecting dots of light off every marbled surface of the room.

I paused every time we neared the side of her room with the mirror. My forehead was almost completely covered in gauze and medical tape.

Maisie, I looked so marvelous that I could barely peel my eyes away.

On the opposite side of the room, we had pasted a map of Dubai on the wall above her desk. I had circled the approximate location of Kiyoma's shop with a big, fat, red marker. Luckily, Al's parents are never too focused on the details of her life.

"First, let's define the problem," said Al.

"We gotta get back to Kiyoma's shop. Without my parents knowing," I said. Kiyoma was the only one who might be willing to tell me more about my real mother.

"Challenges?"

"No car. No driver's license. Not walking distance," I said. Also, I had a cowardly best friend.

"Opportunities?"

I paused. That one had me stumped.

Al smiled.

She picked up a piece of chalk and scribbled three words on the blackboard below the map. She jabbed at each one in turn with her piece of chalk:

Consuela. Taxi. Al.

"This is too easy. Next Saturday morning, you'll come over. We'll tell Consuela we need to go downtown for a social studies project. My parents will never ask. Your parents will never know. Consuela, well, she'll be oblivious, as usual…"

It was a plan. A good one: brilliant, yet simple.

See, Maisie. Finally, we're getting somewhere.

Chapter 6

Use Your Tradecraft

Now, Maisie, you know all about being a spy. But, being a spy's kid, well, that's a different challenge altogether. You can't get too attached. You have to stay flexible, nimble. You have to assimilate. Or you die.

Think I'm being melodramatic? Say, every morning for three years (roughly twenty-three per cent of your life) you use your teaspoon to carefully pick out the decadent white-and-milk chocolate twirls from your chocolate muesli to savor last. And then, one day—Bam!—the twirls are gone. Forever.

Now, you have two choices: 1. Wallow in your longing for twirls, or, 2. Learn how to peel a hot buttery, chocolate croissant one layer at a time, until you finally bite into that strangely delicious chocolate rod in the center....

The point is, Maisie, Candy was so pleased with my assimilating that she barely asked a question the Saturday morning Al and I put our plan into action. Instead, she pulled me into a hug. Her fingers squeezed unnaturally into my back.

"Honey, you do me proud. You know that, right?"

I struggled to breathe. The smell of hairspray and perfume overpowered me at this close distance, but I endured it with dignity.

"I know it's been a tough year. Lots of change. Lots of news. Well, you've thrived anyways, you gorgeous daughter of mine."

She released me at last, nipping me once on the nose with her thumb. I avoided her eyes and instead stared at the neckline of her lime-green dress.

Yes, excitement pulsed through me like a white tornado. I was on the verge of discovering my innate capacity for international crime, or, possibly, computer hacking. The varied possibilities took on a physical presence in my mind— buzzing and humming and making me dizzy with all the potential. My potential.

But, truth be told, something painful radiated on the right side of my head. I had run through my reasoning over and over about why I had to know more, but what I was about to do still felt wrong. Black, not white.

Maisie, I hadn't yet assimilated to all the deception.

I raised my guilty eyes to Candy's.

"See you this afternoon, Mom."

With Al and Consuela at my side, the souk looked different. It felt different, too.

I wasn't overwhelmed by the throngs of people, nor by the rich mix of smells and languages that oozed through the alleyways. The heat didn't feel oppressive. Nor did I scuttle away from eager shopkeepers as soon as they turned their attention to me. I watched Al, then mimicked her quick hand motion that signaled—without a word spoken—'do not disturb.'

It is a powerful little thing, that hand motion. It reminded me of something so simple, so innate—like breathing or walking—that I had forgotten all about it: I had the power to make things happen.

There was just one problem: Consuela. Now that she had escorted us to the souk, we needed to lose her, fast. I couldn't trust her with the truth about my mother. My stolen necklace hung around my neck like a noose.

Always Pay Attention. I looked around, jolted myself to a heightened state of awareness.

It was a crowded morning at the souk; a messy jumble of elbows and shoulders. Ahead of us, the alleyway forked into two. To our right, a busy street, lined by parked cars (E72478, E23257, E40603). To our left, wooden abras bobbed in the creek, ferrying tourists and traders, back and forth, across the creek's banks. Consuela shuffled along a few paces behind us, a cell phone clutched in her right hand. Ding. She paused and looked down at her phone.

Don't act weird.

"Hey, Al, I want to find a golden camel," I said, cool as sweet tea.

Al looked at me with narrowed eyes. I nodded towards Consuela.

"Oh, yes. That sounds wonderful. Let's go find a golden camel, Nora."

Ding. Consuela looked down at her phone as she shuffled behind us, matching our progress step-by-step.

Al and I turned right, towards the narrower of the two forks ahead.

A man nearly flattened Al to the ground running after a runaway toddler. Consuela didn't even glance up.

"Where can we find a golden camel, I wonder, Al?"

"Perhaps down this way, Nora."

I paused before a large store that seemed to glow from the inside. "How about this shop, Al?"

'I heart Dubai' shirts, stuffed camels and miniature, neon green Burj Khalifas lined its shelves and filled its carousels. Dozens of tourists pushed against each other inside.

"What a wonderful idea, Nora." We marched towards the store, signaling our intent to enter as clear as a smoke signal. I risked a quick glance behind to assess our status.

Consuela had glanced up as we entered the shop—ding—then had paused just outside the entrance, looking back down at her phone.

Never be predictable.

I yanked Al's arm down, hard, and we both crouched behind a large carousel filled with snow globes. I peeked around the corner. Consuela hadn't noticed that we were out of sight. She took several steps forward, her nose still buried in her phone.

Adrenaline shot through my veins, as we rotated around the carousel, one step at a time, matching Consuela's progress precisely. I prayed that she wouldn't notice our disappearance for just a few moments more…

Just as we had made a full rotation around the carousel and Consuela's wide back faced us like a white flag, we blasted back out of the store. We snaked through the crowds, leapt over one huge pile of rugs, nearly flattened a man in a green polo, and elbowed two old ladies out of the way. We didn't pause before jumping onto an old wooden abra, just as it pulled away from the dock.

Only then, hunched over, panting for air, and steadying myself on the rocking boat, did I turn to see if we had lost

Consuela. I searched the crowds, a single bead of sweat running down my forehead.

"We're black," I said triumphantly. All clear.

I pushed open the door to Kiyoma's shop and paused as my eyes adjusted to the dim lighting inside. Al waved away the dust in front of her face.

"Are you sure this is the place?" she whispered.

I nodded.

Everything inside was exactly as I remembered. Kiyoma's army of elephants lined the shelves. Elephants hung from the ceiling and cascaded down the walls. The single bulb hung from the ceiling, defiantly dark.

But, this time, everything took on a different tint. A darker tint.

The elephants seemed to stare at me ominously, accusingly. My nose tingled with the overwhelming smell of must. A crack in one corner ran from the ceiling nearly down to the floor, giving the place an overwhelming sense of decay.

How had I missed that before?

My hand found its way to the necklace hanging around my neck. I unclasped it and buried it deep in my pocket.

Now that we were here, I realized I wasn't sure what to expect from Kiyoma. She could have called the police. They could be waiting in the shadows to seize my stolen necklace. A chill shot down through my spine. I caught my reflection in a tiny mirror on the wall. I looked so pale I was almost translucent.

"Are you sure?" Al whispered. "This place gives me the creeps."

We heard a shuffle from the back, from behind the beaded curtain. The sound grew louder and inched closer, and Al and I took two steps backward, arms linked. Al placed one hand on the front door, easing it open, ready to run.

"Miss Nora. You've returned," a voice said to our backs, from right outside the front door of the shop.

"Sweet Jemima!" Al screeched, flinging around.

Kiyoma stood before us. In the brilliant light of day, she looked as thin and wispy as a willow branch. A little smile crept onto her face.

"Of course, you did. They said you would," she said.

With all the words to choose from at this crucial moment—all the thoughts and questions that had raced through my head in the early morning when the call to prayers had awakened me and left me restless—my mind had gone blank.

I dug deep. "Yes," I said.

Kiyoma reached across us to push the door open wide.

"Well, then. Come, come. I imagine we have much to discuss."

Chapter 7

Look Around; Everyone Is Suspect

"We don't have much time," I said to Kiyoma.

"Yeah, we're here covertly," Al said, glancing over her shoulder back at the front door.

Kiyoma placed one index finger to her lips. She grabbed keys from the small table near the back carefully as if trying to avoid their jangle, then hurried back to the front door. She didn't speak until we were safely out with the shop locked behind us.

"We can't talk here. It's not...safe," she whispered, looking left and right.

I followed her gaze, scanning the crowds.

No Consuela.

Al shot me a worried look. I shrugged, not seeing any apparent danger in our proximity.

(But I wasn't paying attention, Maisie. Not really. Had I looked more carefully, for example, would I have noticed if one of the men walking to my right was the same that we had passed earlier, by the abras? Well, that we'll never know because I wasn't looking for the right thing. Not yet.)

Kiyoma shot off down the alleyway to the left and Al and I hurtled after her. She hung right, then left, then right, into increasingly narrow spaces turned eerily yellow and blue from the tarps hanging above us. We were wandering deep into the souk; far beyond where snow globes were sold. Al shot me increasingly worried looks, then stopped altogether.

"Where are we going?" she asked. "I'm not exactly comfortable with all this…"

Kiyoma nodded her head to a shop on the left. A shop full of barrels of spices and smoky oud. I stifled a cough at the overwhelming aroma.

"Here. My sister's shop. Where it's safe to talk. Come, come." We watched while she weaved past the barrels to the back corner. She overturned three buckets as seats.

I followed her in and took a seat on the largest of the buckets, splattered with something dark. I squeezed my eyes shut and tried not to think about the fact that we were squeezed here, knees knocking, in the corner of a tiny spice shop in an obscure souk, with a woman I didn't really know.

When I opened them again, Kiyoma was looking at me, eyebrows arched. I knew she expected me to say something. And I knew already that she was uncommonly comfortable with silence.

"I wanted to talk to you about my mother. She disappeared when I was just a baby. When we spoke earlier, well, you implied that I…I sorta just went with it. I'm sorry," I said.

Kiyoma's eyes went soft.

"I see," she said.

My mind bubbled like a cauldron.

"How were you so sure it was my mother who stole your necklace? Couldn't this all be a strange coincidence…?" I trailed off, never realizing before how much I hoped to acquit the mother I never knew.

"What do you know about your mother, Miss Nora?" Kiyoma asked, her voice smooth as glass.

Thief, runaway mom, strange tactical fashion sense.

"Nothing. Nothing at all," I said twice, making the lie blink neon.

"And you have no contact with Natalya? No relationship at all with her?"

"No."

"How interesting," Kiyoma mused. She stared off into space for an excruciatingly long time. I rearranged myself on my bucket. "Well, I'm not sure what help I can be of then. I only met her the one time."

My stomach knotted into a pit. A dead-end, I realized. I had prepared for every possible outcome, except for this one.

"But over the years I've thought a lot about your mother, Miss Nora. How that one meeting changed my life. I was wrong about Natalya once. I could be wrong about her again…" Kiyoma paused, as if she didn't know how to continue. As if she were selecting her words with care. "You should know that she paid me for the necklace. Paid me for the necklace, and then much more. You asked me how I knew it was Natalya. That's how I knew."

My thief-of-a-mother paid Kiyoma back?

Al jabbed me in the ribs, pointing to a scuffle from the front of the shop. I leaned in toward her to see who was upfront.

"But, Miss Nora, there's something else. Something important I must tell you." Kiyoma's piercing eyes collected mine and drew them back to her. "The necklace. I think it's cursed. You have to get rid of it."

Lord.

Al leaned away from me as if to put more distance between us.

"Over the years, I've had time to think about the course of my life, the bad and the good. I've only recently realized that the necklace was cursed. It must have become…warped at some point. And ever since you brought that necklace back into my shop, well, darkness has once again entered my life. People have been visiting me. Threatening me…"

A woman rushed inside, past Al, and bent down to whisper in Kiyoma's ear. Kiyoma's eyes went wide.

"Someone's looking for you, Miss Nora. And they're close. We have to move."

Blessed. Consuela was nearby.

Kiyoma jumped upright and dashed off at a pace that required Al and me to jog behind, dodging bicycles and wheelbarrows and toddlers as we turned right and left and right again. I was nearly knocked over on my back when I bumped shoulders with a tall man in black. When I glanced back, over my shoulder, he shot us a menacing look.

Finally, the alleyways widened. The shops once again sold riffraff, and people in polo shirts took selfies. The elephant shop loomed ahead.

I sprinted up to Kiyoma's side as we neared her shop, an idea taking root.

"How did Natalya do it?" I asked, out of breath. "I mean, how did she pay you back." A lead, possibly.

Kiyoma didn't turn her head toward me, but I could see a tiny smile creep onto her face.

"Are you destined to find your mother, Miss Nora?"

This wasn't a question.

"Wait here. I have one thing for you before you must…go," Kiyoma whispered. She pinned us to the outside window of her shop with one finger, before unlocking the door and rushing inside.

Kiyoma returned with an envelope dangling between her pointer finger and thumb. She handed it to Al before taking both of my hands into hers.

"The money your mother sent saved my daughter's life. I was never able to thank her. When you find her, I need you to thank her, Miss Nora. For me. Will you do that?"

"Ever heard of a place called Opelousas?" Al asked, reading the return address on the letter.

Opelousas?

Kiyoma yanked me closer, so close that I could smell black tea hot on her breath. "But, Miss Nora, you must listen. Carefully. You have to get rid of the necklace. Before you bring more darkness upon both of us. You understand?"

I nodded, but at this close distance, I was certain Kiyoma could see my lie.

There was no way would I get rid of the one thing linking me to my real mother.

And, I couldn't lie well. Not yet.

I nodded again.

Kiyoma released my hands, shaking her head. "Then please don't come back here again. Not ever."

I swung toward Al to swipe the envelope from her hands and looked down, prepared to find what I knew was obvious—after all, what else is in Opelousas?

Sure enough: The address was Grandmamma Aurelia's. Even expecting this, I was stunned.

"Miss Alexandra! Miss Nora!" a voice shouted from across the street.

Consuela.

Kiyoma stepped back into the shadow of her doorway, arms crossed.

Poor Consuela stumbled as she jogged across the street, her face dripping with sweat and black mascara-laced tears.

"Miss Alexandra! Miss Nora! You run away! I look for you in every single shop, down every street. You make me more angrier than ever before. I nearly call the police."

She pulled Al into a tight embrace, wiping her tears with the back of her hand. Then, she dug her fingers into my arm, yanking me forward, away from Kiyoma and her strange elephant shop and all that she knew about my mother.

I resisted Consuela's pull. I wasn't done: I needed to know more. But Consuela was insistent and angry and Al seemed intent on going along.

I looked back as we were swept away—for ever, I knew even then. But Kiyoma had already disappeared. Her shop was dark and a *CLOSED* sign swung gently from the door handle.

My cursed, stolen necklace weighed heavy in my pocket. That's when one additional thought hit me like a ton of bricks: Grandmamma Aurelia wasn't even a blood relation. Not really.

And she had lied, too.

Chapter 8

The Truth Can Hurt

I knew I was going to be in trouble when I arrived back home.

I had brainstormed the entire taxi ride, tuning out Consuela and Al's squawking. I pressed my forehead against the window as the glittering skyscrapers whipped by, trying to think of something—anything—that could explain why I had run away from Consuela in the souk.

But I found no alibi. Not a credible one anyways.

So, several minutes later, when Consuela deposited me at my villa with a stern look and crossed arms, I told the truth. My head hung so low it nearly mopped the kitchen floor.

"That will be all, Consuela. We'll take it from here," Candy said. The door slammed shut, and my heart dropped into my stomach. I braced myself for yelling, a grounding, a possible forced commitment to a debutante ball.

What I received was even worse: Silence.

At last, after enduring as much as I could bear, I lifted my eyes from the floor to face the prosecution. Candy stood still, her eyes fixed on Dad. Her blank face—wiped clean of her perky smile—looked pale and skeletal.

A shiver ran down my spine for the second time that day.

"Well, what did you learn about Natalya, honey?" Candy asked, low and slow.

"Grandmamma knows, I think. About the stolen necklace. About Natalya, too. That's all, really…"

I trailed off, uncertain. The bit about the possible curse was more than I figured they could handle at the moment.

"I see."

The silence returned.

"And what is your plan, honey?" Candy's voice dripped like honey, an eerie contrast to the hard-boiled expression on her face.

She was definitely laying a trap for me. Caution blinked like hazard lights in my mind. But I was still hard-wired for truth and before I could check myself, I had forged ahead, directly into the minefield….

"I need to find her," I whispered. "I need to know more about her."

(I know, Maisie! I know!)

"Walter, darling?" Candy said grimly.

She turned to look out the window, to the dunes beyond, her slender arms crossed tightly, as if she were hugging herself. What was going through her head, Lord only knew. But for reasons that I couldn't quite pinpoint, I had a sense that her anger wasn't directed toward me.

Dad hadn't moved from the kitchen table, where he cradled his head in his hands. But, after I spoke, he turned his big, disappointed eyes toward me.

"Nora Jean, I think it's time you and I went for a drive."

We had driven only twenty minutes, but we were already out past the mall and skyscrapers, the tidy new housing developments and, finally, the last of the construction vehicles. We were headed straight into the desert.

"Look, Dad…"

"Shh." He put his fingers to his lips, then pointed to the roof of the car. I looked up, squinting, but could see nothing there.

We exited the highway, bumped over a camel grate and drove off the road. He got out and walked a dune away. Considering my options, not knowing what else to do, I followed.

For a while, we both stood, silent, looking out across the sea of white. The pale-grey sky bled into the sand, blurring the horizon. I felt as if I were looking into the abyss—a stark, terrifying, beautiful abyss.

"There's a bug in the car. A listening device," Dad said. "There is one in the house, too. Not sure where. Lord knows I've surveyed the premises."

Dad turned to look at me, his brow creased, hands stuffed in his pockets.

"Now I don't want you to be worried about it, darling. Standard procedure for the CIA. For our own protection, really. But you need to be aware because I need to tell you something that's…that's not authorized. Something we can't talk about aloud. Ever. At least not in the house or car or in public or in the presence of any kind of cellular device…"

The list grew long. I turned to look back at our spy-mobile, only now understanding why we were here in the desert, a dune away from the car. Among only sand and beetles and silence.

"I trust you, Nora Jean. Beyond your years. And I get why you want to know more about Natalya. I do. But this ain't a game…"

"…it's not a game! She's my mother." I spat my words at him.

He wiped his brows clean, turned back to the dunes. I had never before noticed the grey hair around his temples, nor the lines around his eyes and mouth, now plain as day in the brilliant light of the desert. Dad had always been large and loud and also a bit ridiculous. I had never before seen him look so, well, tired.

"What I mean to say is that this is complicated. Dangerous. More than your mother knows. More than Grandmamma knows. More than anyone else knows but me. And now, you."

More complicated than thief, runaway mom, and accursed?

"Natalya was a Russian spy. Is a Russian spy, I surmise. I'm not permitted to know. I only met Natalya because I was directed to. She was a target of interest to the United States government."

Hiccup.

Yes, more complicated.

"Lord, I loved that woman something fierce, even though it wasn't…authorized. Maybe, because it wasn't authorized. A terrible weakness on my part. The devil doing his dirty work, so to speak. And it came with consequences. Dire consequences, darling."

Hiccup.

"Thirteen years ago, I had a difficult choice laid out in front of me. My livelihood, family, country, everything I hold dear in life. Or Natalya. Well, it wasn't much of a decision, really. I had to give her up and...take you away from her. Protect you from her, so to speak."

He turned back to face me, but his eyes were above me, somewhere I couldn't reach them—up and to the left, Maisie.

Hiccup.

"Darling, Natalya is part of an elite Russian squad of assassins. She could have killed us both. She probably was planning to all along, hard though it was for me to comprehend at the time..."

All around us, the desert buzzed. A beetle crawled onto my foot and clung. I cast it away, irritated.

Hiccup.

"But, Grandmamma Aurelia...?" My head had fogged up thick with questions. Did I speak Russian?

"Grandmamma doesn't know any of this! You are not to tell her. Or anyone." Dad's voice turned from baritone to bass. A commandment.

I turned away from Dad to the desert, trying to clear the fog. But the fog only thickened.

Was I a natural with weapons?

"Lord knows, I nearly lost my job over Natalya once. I could easily lose it for real this time."

Hiccup.

Was I—gulp—a natural born killer?

"But, even more troubling, darling, is the danger. There are people out there, bad people, looking for Natalya. Or working with Natalya. Or working against Natalya. Or pretending to work against Natalya. It's always a bit...murky...in this business."

I looked down at my hands, so pale and smooth. Were they capable of pulling a trigger or closing around someone's neck?

"I'm asking you to do something difficult, darling girl. Lord knows, this whole situation stung me hard long ago. But I have no other choice. Drop this. Please." His whisper came out sharp as if he were etching his words onto a rock.

I looked at Dad, scanned him head to toe. His face had creased into lines—the lines of a hundred years of worries.

Suddenly, the fog cleared. The truth washed over me. My real mother was a Russian spy and an assassin. She probably planned to kill Dad. And/or me.

Also, I could tell no one.

The reality was so marvelous that a single tear escaped my right eye, rolled down my cheek, and dripped down into the sand. The faint circle of water evaporated in an instant.

Thing is, Maisie, Dad was right: So-far, this had been a game to me. A silly, dangerous, little child's game. My chin fell so far it down it nearly knocked into my chest.

"Okay," I whispered. "Got it."

In the silence of the desert, my words clapped like thunder.

Chapter 9

Be Aware of Your Limitations; Play to Your Strengths

Maisie, you should know that this story almost ended there.

My cheeks burned whenever I thought about my antics at the souk. How adorable was it that I tried to chase down the trail of my real mother? My mother, who, by the way, is a KGB assassin.

I wasn't clever, Maisie, I was just a stupid kid. And finally, I knew it.

So, I tried my best to focus not on Natalya, but what was directly in front of me—Dad, Candy, Grandmamma, and my global nomad life. And, there, I found something warm and familiar. Cozy, even.

Yet.

And, yet…

What I'm trying to say, Maisie, is that the story did not end there after all.

"So?" Al whispered into the phone the morning after our shenanigans at the souk. I sat cross-legged on my bed, behind a closed door.

"I'm practically grounded for life," I lied. Truth was, I had grounded myself. "You?"

"Nada."

"Wait. What?" I asked, shocked.

"Yeah. Consuela has a soft spot for lost mother situations. She didn't tell my parents. I'm off the hook."

I pulled the phone down to my lap for a moment before returning it to my ear.

This was what was wrong with children these days. At least, that's what Grandmamma would say.

"Well, good," I said.

"So, what's the plan now?" she whispered.

"The plan?"

"Tracking your mom. I was thinking we should start by googling the address on the envelope…"

"…Stop. Please. I'm done with that whole thing."

I heard a rustling on the other end of the line as if Al were getting up or flailing her hands. I braced myself.

"That whole thing? You mean to say that now, after you've discovered a possible curse, after we finally have an actionable lead, you're giving up?" Her outrage shot through the phone at me and stung. I was glad to be at a safe distance.

"Yes," I whispered.

I heard only silence on the other end of the line.

"You feeling okay, Curly?" Her voice had gone soft.

"I'm fine. I'm good. Good. Just don't want to talk about it."

I glanced up at the mirror across from my bed, considered my reflection in the mirror. I didn't recognize the girl I saw there: so young, a little nicked-up. Since when did my perfect nose angle slightly to the left? I forced myself to look away from this eerie Picasso version of myself.

"Okay…but first—what are you going to do with the necklace? I mean, not to be rude, but I'm entering the prime of my life and I have to know about any potential curses…"

"…It's gone," I said, lying for the third time in approximately twenty-three seconds.

A pang of guilt pulsed through me, but then—surprisingly—dripped away leaving me feeling light, free.

I smiled.

I may have been a stupid kid, Maisie. But I was something else, too—something important. And deception coursed through my blood.

As my mind churned, the weeks rolled forward through autumn and halfway into November, and at long last, the ferocious Arabian heat loosened its grip on Dubai.

One evening—Thursday—as I walked home from school, the wind picked up and the sun dipped low, bouncing its light off a million glittering grains of sand. The whole city turned golden. I threw my hands out and my head back to savor the moment.

Finally, I understood the appeal of the place.

Also, I no longer yearned for my not-really home.

"Oh, is it sleeting there again?" I savagely asked Grandmamma over the phone. I took my new, enormous, tortoise-shell-rimmed sunglasses out of my backpack and pushed them onto my nose. "The weather here is perfect every day. Actually, all the sunshine is a little boring."

Fortunately, Al had earned the leading role in the middle school play, a starting position on the middle school soccer team and a spot on the honor roll. With all of her achievements, she couldn't possibly be a bad influence on me, despite what happened at the souk. Dad and Candy agreed.

So, that Thursday evening, a couple of hours after I arrived home, a white, vintage Land Rover rolled into the driveway of our villa, honking.

"*Yallah, yallah*!" Al hollered. "Let's go."

I announced my exit to Candy as I raced out the door but screeched to a halt when Al came into view. She had wrapped a red-checked scarf around her head, Bedouin-style and was sitting in the open back of the Land Rover, arms splayed wide.

"This is ridiculous." I pointed to her head, then circled my finger to encompass her whole being.

You should know that Al's family is from Ireland, via New Jersey.

"Oh, *habibi, habibi…*" she said.

Poor Consuela waved, her head also wrapped up Bedouin-style.

Al's parents, Barb and Stewie, glanced up at me from the front. Both nodded, then immediately returned to typing on their phones.

"Miss Nora, sit beside me," Consuela said, gently patting an empty space beside her.

I sighed. Ever since the incident at the souk and Al's explanation to her afterward, Consuela had taken a special interest in me. She shot me pitiful looks from across the room and gave me awkward and unsolicited hugs.

Lord knows, Maisie, the last thing I needed in my life at the moment was another not-really-mother figure.

I shot Al a glare as I climbed up into the back to the space beside Consuela.

At last, just as the sun dipped below the horizon, we pulled into camp.

A bonfire burned bright in the center, making everything glow amber—the ornate red carpets covering the sand, the low pillows and the torches leading to the black sea of sand and stars surrounding us. Smoke filled the air and Arabian music oozed from near a tent on one side, where two camels were tied.

Other groups of people lounged back on low pillows, having clearly arrived in camp before us. They drank coffee and spoke in animated voices, their faces golden from the fires around us. A man in a green shirt held his cell phone high above him, taking a video of the whole scene.

"So, Nora, I understand your family is quite new to Dubai?" Barb asked politely, rearranging herself on the carpet. Some people are just not built to sit on the ground.

"Oh, no, we've been here for years. I was born here, actually," I lied. I'm not sure why.

Al's head shot up.

"Ah, so then you must know if this is a *Medjool* or a *Dabbas*? This is much tastier than what we normally eat at home…" She turned to spit something into the sand beside us, then wiped her spittle with the back of her hand.

"Yes, Curly, please teach us all you know about…dates," Al said, narrowing her eyes at the wrinkled piece of food she held between her thumb and pointer finger.

I shot her an icy stare.

Luckily, the music grew loud, and everyone hushed. A gnarled old woman emerged from the tent, covered head-to-toe in black. From where I sat, her abaya looked as though it were embroidered with a thousand gold cobras. Hunched forward and leaning sideways into her dark cane, she took one painful step after another toward the bonfire.

The pace of the music increased. The woman threw her cane aside and lost her hunch. She shook her hips, her arms twisting around her body like snakes. Just as she drew close— close enough that we could see her dark eyes through the slits in her sheila—she flung off her abaya.

To my surprise, a young woman stood before us. Gold crisscrossed her bare belly and jangled with each gyration of her hips. A mane of shiny, black hair cascaded halfway down her back and danced with her every move. Even from a distance, I could smell her woody, sweet scent.

It must have been jasmine, I remember thinking. Absolutely everything about her made me think of jasmine.

Maisie, this strange place has taught me one thing: a particular beauty lies in things that are hidden.

"Grab food, girls. Before it's all gone," Barb whispered, jolting me back to reality.

The music slowed once again, and the young woman started her slow dance back to the tent.

I lingered a second longer, transfixed. When I finally got up and walked towards the grill, my neck prickled with the sense that I had picked up a tail. I swung around.

Actually, I was red hot.

"Miss Nora." Consuela stood before me, six inches into my personal space.

I resisted the urge to groan. I had zero interest in talking with anyone about my maternal situation, least of all Consuela. But, here in the middle of the deep, dark desert, there was no escape.

"I have something for you." Consuela handed me a folded sheet of paper, grinning. On it, Consuela had neatly written out an email address. Kiyoma's email address.

"But, how? Why?" I asked, surprised.

"I went back to the souk, Miss Nora. For you. I know you in real trouble with your parents. But, if you want to find out about your mother, you should be able to know. Maybe this will help."

"Oh, Consuela. I can't—I'm done," I said, shaking my head.

The music had stopped, and from where we stood, I could see the young belly dancer behind the tent, pulling on her abaya. She glared at me when we locked eyes. Stung, I turned away.

"But, why, Miss Nora? Why now you not want to know about your mother?"

"Because she…left." I grimaced. What else could I say? I couldn't tell Consuela that she possibly wanted to kill me. And/or Dad. Or that she was a KGB assassin.

"I left, too," Consuela said. "I had to, or else my children would starve."

I turned back to her, surprised by these words.

"You have kids?" I asked.

(Truth be told, Maisie—I had never even thought to ask.)

"Three of them. Ten, six and two years old." Consuela wiped away a single tear with the back of her hand. "I haven't seen them in over a year."

Two years old?

"Miss Nora, where I come from, things not so easy. Where I come from, love sometimes is…money for rice.

Money for the doctor. But, still, someday I hope my children want to know about me, too. Just like you with your mother."

Scenes flashed through my mind. Consuela's incessant text messaging. Consuela staring at photos on her phone, as if lost in another world. Consuela carefully counting each dirham change that we flung at her after she treated us to ice cream sandwiches on Al's birthday...

Consuela was supporting her own children, linked to her across the earth by only the screen of her phone. Meanwhile, Al and I had mocked her poor grammar.

The shameful reality punched me in the gut.

"If your mother left, she must have had good reason. That's what I say." Consuela's voice came out sharp. Her eyes had turned to steel. A different woman stood in front of me—a stronger one—as if she, too, had cast off an abaya.

Before I could consider my actions, my right hand reached out for hers. I gave it a squeeze. A hand hug.

(Yes, Maisie, a hand hug.)

Consuela was a daily figure in my life, but still, I had gotten her all wrong. I had become so focused on myself that I hadn't even been paying attention to those around me.

What else had I missed?

I tried to dam the flood, push the thoughts back out of my mind and stay focused on the cozy life in front of me. But I failed. Something nagged. A question that turned over and over in my mind the rest of that evening—through dinner, the long drive back home and while I lay in bed, restless and unable to sleep.

If Natalya was a cold-hearted assassin who had planned to kill me, why had she stolen Kiyoma's necklace—for me?

And, with that question, another: and, if Grandmamma knew nothing of what Dad had told me in the desert, what was her part in this story?

The image of the belly dancer casting off her abaya haunted my thoughts.

Who was Natalya under the veil?

Who was *I*?

The fog only lifted for a moment—just enough for me to see one thing plain as day: I was missing something. Something critical. But, what?

Then, the fog socked me in once again.

The next morning, I was bleary from lack of sleep. But I had made my decision. (A small decision, Maisie, but a critical one.)

I clutched my cup of hot cocoa at the kitchen table while Candy prepared pancakes and Dad read Gulf News. I fixed my thoughts on yawning—and yawned—summoning my best impression of a thirteen-year-old without a care in the world.

"Hey, Mom, Dad. So, I was thinking. Winter break is three weeks long. What do you think about visiting Grandmamma this year? I'm sure she'd love the company. Plus, I miss her."

I twirled a strand of hair around one finger.

(You see, Maisie—improvement! Because there was one thread here that I could pull. One thread that didn't involve the CIA or the KGB or Dad possibly losing his job. A thread that dangled loose down in Opelousas, painting alligators onto tiny jewelry boxes.)

Dad pulled the newspaper down to look at me over the top. I shot him my best smile, teeth and all.

"I think that's a wonderful idea. What do you think, Candy?"

I held my breath, a pulse of electricity running from the top of my head down to the tips of my toes.

"Christmas with Mamma," said Candy, looking wistfully through the window at the dunes beyond. "I'll look into tickets today."

I exhaled.

Part Two
Black River

Chapter 10

Trust Your Instincts

One month and one day later, we made our way across the globe from Dubai to Louisiana in three consecutively smaller jets. At last, when we stepped off the third and final plane into the arctic tundra of a Louisiana December, the cold socked me in the face and left me gasping for air. My teeth chattered the whole walk from the airport terminal to the rental car kiosk, and again, as we circled the car lot twice, trying to locate our purple rental Kia.

How people could survive in such conditions, Lord only knew.

I pressed my forehead against the cold glass of the car window while I endured the final leg of our journey—the drive from Lafayette to Opelousas—my hot breath creating semicircles of fog that I wiped clean every couple of minutes. We had taken this drive on many occasions—twice a year, at least—but with each new move across the globe, I saw the place with new eyes.

Also, billboards in Louisiana are even better than newspapers.

The Piggly Wiggly had survived Walmart's arrival. Cheerleaders in Lafayette had won the state championship. A long white-bearded Catholic priest, Father Mac McNaster, was still the poster boy for the annual Zydeco festival. And the most prestigious private school in the area—Opelousas Catholic—was raising funds by raffling off guns.

Lord. It felt good to be home.

Finally, after driving through historic Opelousas, ten minutes south of town, then past an impenetrable pine forest, we turned up the long drive to Grandmamma's estate. The car wheels crunched over gravel as we rolled past the twenty gnarled oaks lining her drive. Christmas wreaths hung from each of her twelve windows. Garland circled each of her six columns, thick as tree trunks.

My heart thumped. Black River had always been a grand dame, Maisie, but, that day, she was looking especially fine.

"Y'all made it. And right on time," a voice rang out, just as I opened the car door.

Grandmamma Aurelia stood in the doorway, her grey hair cascading down past the neckline of her sweater. Her long skirt embroidered with—was it really? Yes—camels waved in the breeze.

Grandmamma has always believed in dressing for the occasion.

She swept down the stairs and pulled me into a fierce hug, before releasing me to embrace Candy and Dad.

"I'm so tickled y'all thought to come this year, of all years." Grandmamma's eyes went misty.

"Momma, you're looking awfully…thin," Candy said, holding her by the shoulders and looking her up and down.

"It's all the yoga, sugar," Grandmamma said wiping her eyes, then placing her palms together into an elegant namaste.

"Oh, oh! The girls are here now. Book club. I planned this perfectly. Come, come."

She clapped her hands twice, then, with a flick of her wrist signaled for us to forget about our luggage and biological necessities, and follow her inside, through the foyer, past the imperial split staircase and into the parlor.

"Ladies, ladies. I told y'all, had a little surprise up my sleeves today," she announced just as we entered, pausing a moment to open her arms wide for dramatic effect. "Let me introduce you to my real-life, blood-relative, Arabians."

Above the antique floors and Persian rugs, perched on chaise and chintz and chesterfield, twelve women squealed. They wore turbans and gold chains, saris and togas, and clutched twelve glasses of bubbly champagne.

"Nora, Walter, Candy, let me introduce you to the fine ladies of the Opelousas book club. This month's choice was Lawrence of Arabia, so the girls have oodles of questions for all y'all about life in the…exotic east."

I leaned close to Dad, his Eau de Airplane tickling my nose.

"Isn't that a movie?" I whispered.

He nodded, grimacing.

"We only watch movies made from books," Grandmamma whispered. "Unless, of course, it's one of the classics…"

Grandmamma ushered us to a cozy seat near the Turkish delights before the inhabitants of the room launched questions at us rapid-fire.

"Thank goodness you're home safe, what with all the terrorists over there. Have you seen an actual terrorist?" the turban asked.

"How do you stand not driving?" the sari asked of Candy.

"Nora, how does it feel to wear…you know…the veil?" the toga whispered.

Well.

Thankfully, after less than an hour, I managed to escape to my room and crawled into bed. Just before surrendering to sleep, a light knock on the door startled me back awake.

"Come in," I groaned, pushing myself back upright.

Grandmamma swept into the room, her long skirt swishing with each step. She took a seat on the side of my bed, her grin stretching as wide as the Mississippi.

"But, Grandmamma, your club?"

"Oh, sugar, they get on just fine without me. They always do. You though, I don't get enough of. And I have something, something I've been waiting to give to you for a long, long time…"

She patted the box she had on her lap, wrapped in a small velveteen sheet.

"…I know you don't remember your Mimi, God rest her soul. But she loved you something fierce. When you were only a few months old, she'd plop you on her lap and sing you her lullabies with that world-famous voice. Amazing Grace, usually. I'm sure your dad has told you all this already…"

Truth was, Dad rarely talked about his late mother. Whenever I asked, he usually mumbled and removed himself from the room. And I never pressed. How could I miss something I didn't remember having?

"When Mimi and I were young mammas, we always dreamed that our babies would get on, that we would live to see the day our babies had babies. But it came late, nearly too late for Mimi. Still, she was sure over the moon when you

72

arrived here in Opelousas, a bundle of fat rolls and black curls."

Grandmamma nipped me on the nose, just like she has since as far back as I can remember.

My weary mind wasn't able to calculate what time it was in Dubai or Opelousas. Nevertheless, my body screamed for sleep and I could think of almost nothing else…

"I promised Mimi that I would give this to you when the time came, sugar. Something that's been passed down woman-to-woman through the generations. And, as her dear friend, as your Grandmamma, it's an honor to do it on her behalf."

She handed me the box delicately as if it contained within it the crown jewels. I unwrapped it, slowly.

Inside, the box was lined with velvet and a diamond tiara sat in the center. When I looked up, I saw that Grandmamma's face shimmered with tiny rainbows.

"Mimi wore this on her wedding day. She always dreamed that you would too someday, sugar."

I smiled, waiting for her to continue. Waiting for her to explain why she was giving this gift to me now, when I was jet-lagged, plane-dirty, and decidedly thirteen years old. But she didn't. She just looked at me as if she expected me to drop over dead with joy.

I picked up the tiara, examining it from all sides.

Well. It certainly wouldn't match anything in my current wardrobe…

"Thank you, Grandmamma. This is so special," I lied. Truth was, I couldn't bear to disappoint her. Even though I was hardwired for deception. Even though she wasn't even a blood relative.

I snapped the box closed, gave her a long hug and excused myself to sleep. And when I laid back to rest, counting the things that I currently needed as much as the diamond tiara sitting beside me on the nightstand (an elephant, a kidney transplant), sleep nearly overtook me…

Well, almost. There was just one thought that slipped into my mind and stuck: Why did Grandmamma seem different on this visit? Just a touch more emotional. Just a sprinkle more sentimental.

But that question, Maisie, just like all the others I was there to unravel, would have to wait for another full rotation of the Earth on its axis.

Chapter 11

Try Elicitation as a First Resort

I awoke fifteen hours later, took a deep breath of Cajun air, and smiled at the calls of the white-fronted geese outside my window. Just like the geese so far from their icy home, I felt a world away from Dubai and all my problems there. Plus, the smell of something hot and buttery floated up from downstairs, beckoning …

But just as my bare toes hit the cold wooden floor, I was shocked wide awake by a realization. All of my unanswered questions had followed me across two continents and an ocean. I was here in Opelousas for a reason. That very day, I would start unravelling the mystery of Grandmamma and Natalya.

I entered the kitchen, following the smell—buttermilk biscuits filled with jam, Lord have mercy—and watched Grandmamma like a hawk would a mouse. She scurried over the checkerboard floor in her butterfly-embroidered overalls. She poured hot coffee into mugs, pulled biscuits out of the oven and fried bacon thin and nearly black, just as Dad likes it.

Candy never eats. But she had a satisfied look on her face as she sipped Grandmamma's world-famous chicory coffee, both hands cupped around her mug. Her eyes had glossed over as she stared out the window at all that green. Well, brown/green. She was not to be disturbed.

Neither was Dad, who barely looked up at me when I entered; he was too busy shoveling biscuits and bacon into his mouth. A spot of grease had blossomed conspicuously right where his stomach protruded. He paused to dab it with a balled-up paper napkin, his chin folding into about two dozen rolls.

And, there, Maisie, was my only living blood relative, save for a Russian assassin.

Should I corner Grandmamma and ask her directly about Natalya? That had to be a last resort. I couldn't trust that she would keep our conversation secret from her only daughter.

Grandmamma plopped a plate of biscuits and bacon in front of me, then shot me a lovely smile.

But how else could I unravel the mystery?

I placed one long piece of bacon into my mouth and *mmmm'ed* my approval.

An idea took root.

"Grandmamma, are you still making your jewelry boxes?" I asked smoothly.

"Oh, sugar. I'll be making those little boxes till the day I die. It's the only purpose of me being on this earth at my ripe old age. That, and the painting, of course."

Grandmamma smiled at her magnum opus—a painting of a one-eyed gator chasing a child.

"I was thinking, maybe I'd like to help you make a jewelry box. For Christmas," I said.

I needed Grandmamma alone, and I knew neither Dad nor Candy would trek up the three flights of stairs, climb one narrow ladder and then shimmy through a two-foot-square hole, into Grandmamma's attic studio.

According to Grandmamma, creating art, like evaluating one's reflection in the mirror, is best done in private.

"Well, sugar, it would be a real treat to create some art with you. Come on now, finish up your breakfast, and I'll take you on up this morning before the party…"

Half an hour later, Grandmamma and I sat perched on two stools high up in the attic—my favorite place in the whole of Black River. The attic was a massive room that spanned the entire footprint of the house. Racks of clothing covered half of the room—Grandmamma's vast and eccentric wardrobe— and her studio spanned the other. Four windows let in four rays of light, speckled with dust.

When I was little—spinning around and around the attic, clutching in my hand the tail end of one of her elegant gowns—I used to make believe that I was the lady of the house, dancing at one of Black River's world-famous balls.

You must understand, Maisie, that at some point in my life a hint was dropped and then my heart clenched onto the idea and wouldn't let go: Black River would, someday, be mine.

The estate has been in the family for generations. My great-great-great-grandmother, Mary Jane, originally purchased the estate when her husband died and left her with a fortune. She passed Black River down to my great-great-grandmother Doris, who expanded it after she set the world on fire by inventing smudge-proof lipstick. Doris then left it to her daughter, Eleanore, who had, as the story goes, the entire attic space converted to a potions laboratory as a child, and then grew up to be a famous chemist. And, finally Eleanore gave it to Grandmamma Aurelia, who had never lived a day in her life outside of iron-clad gates, but whose paintings were sold for thousands of dollars to wealthy Yankee clients all the way up in Manhattan.

I followed Grandmamma's brush strokes precisely. We were working on a variation of her top seller: the painted Alligator Lady, a Christmas special.

"Grandmamma, I wanted to ask you something. For a friend," I began.

Grandmamma mumbled approval as she added the final details to the tiny baby Jesus cradled in the Alligator's claws.

"My friend recently found out that her mother isn't really her real mother, and she really wants to find out more about her," I said.

"Who's 'her'?"

"The real mother."

Grandmamma nodded, switching to a red brush and then adding lipstick to the Alligator's gaping jaws. I continued.

"The problem is, her parents don't want her to know any more about her real mother because, well, she might not be a good person."

"So the real mother's parents don't want your friend to find her?"

"No, the not-really mother."

"So, the real mother's grandmother is a bad person?"

"No, the real mother."

"I'm confused, sugar."

I set down my brush, dug my elephant necklace out of my pocket and dropped it on the table. It landed with a thud.

"Where did you get this, Grandmamma?"

Grandmamma glanced at the necklace briefly, before switching to yet another brush. With several elegant strokes, a beautiful Star of David took shape above the Alligator's right shoulder.

"I found that at a little antique store downtown. Tiny's Antiques right there on Broad Street, next to the hardware store. According to Tiny, it's at least one hundred years old. Probably brought over here to Cajun country by French Canadian traders of fur and tobacco…"

Without even a pause, she prattled on with a history of the necklace that brimmed with unnecessary detail, trivia, fiddle-faddle, nonsense.

What I'm trying to say, Maisie, is that Grandmamma's lies blinked neon. Finally, I was paying attention.

(I know you are, too.)

A flash of heat crept up my neck to my face as I watched Grandmamma put the final touches on her jewelry box.

Truth is, her jewelry boxes have always been odd. I just never had the heart to admit it before.

Maisie, I hope now you can understand why one hour and forty-two minutes later, I found myself alone, on all fours, crouched behind Grandmamma's vast walnut desk, with a flashlight and a slender screwdriver in hand. But while the former was useful (I had kept the lights off for cover), the latter was unnecessary: Grandmamma's files were unlocked, organized, and ready for her someday-biographer.

What was I looking for exactly? I couldn't say then, and I can't say now. I suppose when my attempts at elicitation had failed, I saw no other option. It was a long shot, but, perhaps, hidden among her files, was something that would explain why Grandmamma had sent money to Kiyoma for my stolen necklace. Perhaps I would find something that would explain what Grandmamma knew about Natalya.

Preparations for the annual Black River Christmas Gala were furiously underway outside the heavy closed door of Grandmamma's office. The buzz of activity had, at least so far, allowed me to slip away undiscovered. I could hear the rustling of various evergreens and the tinkling of bells and lights, all finding their way from their dusty boxes in the attic, to the main floor.

I began my subterfuge.

I tore through the dentist appointments, tax returns and letters of the 1990s. I eased up on the speed as I reached the files of early 2000s, finding more newspaper articles and doctor's appointments. I heard *Joy to the World* blast from the stereo system just as I started on the files from 2010. I knew Candy would be looking for me soon to dress for the party.

"Nora? Nora!" called Candy from somewhere upstairs.

Blessed.

I yanked out the rest of Grandmamma's files, and with my thumb, flipped through them to triage the final few minutes of my search. Just as I was about to abandon hope, I found a curious thing: an undated manilla envelope, taped closed.

"Nora! Where are you?" Candy yelled, her voice inching downwards and closer by the minute.

I paused for a moment to consider the ramifications. I had no cover for action; no alibi once the envelope was torn open. But I had to know what was inside. I just had to, Maisie.

I dropped my flashlight and ripped it open. I picked up the flashlight to read the words, willing them to reveal something about Natalya and Grandmamma and, with luck, me.

But the words were not what I expected—not at all.

I didn't understand all of Grandmamma's medical report, but two words beamed at me clear as day:

Terminal Cancer.

Chapter 12

But a Confrontation
May Be Necessary

Several minutes later, Candy prattled on with a list of the names of all the relatives, friends and acquaintances I would be expected to remember at the Black River Christmas Gala. Her hands twisted my hair into two tortuous braids as she outlined their new babies, gallbladder surgeries, football scholarships and vacations to Savannah.

Truth be told, I didn't hear a thing.

Grandmamma had cancer.

Grandmamma had *cancer*.

Even repeating the words inside my head wouldn't dislodge whatever was stuck there. I should have been sad, or, perhaps, hurt.

What I should not be feeling was nothing.

I craned my head, pulling against Candy's grip, to look out the window of her childhood room, over the vast front drive of Black River. Grandmamma's live oaks stood in a tidy line along the drive. I couldn't help but think of the lazy summer days I spent climbing their branches one by one and then swinging my legs until my feet tingled.

But, on this day, the sky was the color of gunmetal. And the oaks' branches looked twisted, like a row of gnarled witches' hands.

What kind of person had I become? Why wasn't I feeling...anything?

A light drizzle started to patter against the windowsill.

I turned away, to watch Candy in the mirror as she pinned two enormous bows at the end of each braid and then used a battalion of bobby pins to calm my curls. She smiled and hummed as she worked, her hands moving with medical precision.

There was no way she knew.

And Dad, who had spent the previous hour in the parlor skimming *The Evolution of Bees*?

No, I alone knew the terrible news.

Finished, Candy beamed at my reflection in the mirror. When I took in the sight, I scowled.

I was the daughter of a spy and an assassin, apparently incapable of normal human feeling. In all likelihood, deception, coercion and a killer instinct pulsed through my veins. One would think that this entitled me to pass on the red, monogrammed Christmas dress.

Alas. According to Candy, suffering is an essential part of beauty.

Dressed and presentable, I stood at the foot of the staircase ready to welcome our guests. But my attention was elsewhere: on Grandmamma. And, that day, my eyes burned at her like lasers.

She swished about in her long, green, velvet dress covered in pins and bows and shaped to look like a Christmas tree. She poured her attention into the placement of the candles, the orientation of the silver serving ware and the timing of the carving of the roast.

And when the guests poured in—a jumble of fascinators, bowties and babies in knee-high socks—I watched as she floated from group to group, talking about new hunting rifles and home renovations, and politely removing herself from any whisper of Yankees or Democrats.

Her laugh, as usual, sounded a little like clinking wine glasses. Joyful, light. And her head tilted backward as if she were launching her happiness like bubbles across the room.

There was no sign of the sickness that was rotting her from within.

There was no sign that all this around us, all this joy, was a lie.

At long last, she excused herself to check in with the kitchen.

I pounced as soon as the kitchen door swung shut, enclosing us in a steamy room full of hired staff.

"You have cancer," I stated, plain as day.

The room went silent.

Grandmamma turned to look at me, her eyes wide.

"Sugar?"

"You lied about it, too. Just like everything else." I hurled my words at her, surprising even myself with their force.

With the back of my hand, I wiped a bit of spittle that had been thrust out of my mouth.

Perhaps I did feel something after all.

The kitchen staff looked around for the nearest exit. None found, they absorbed themselves in their duties, pretending not to be engraving each word into their memory.

I came closer to Grandmamma, the smocking on my dress allowing me to march with long, menacing steps.

"You lied about my necklace, my mother and now your cancer. Is anything you say true, Grandmamma?"

She flinched, then grabbed a discarded doily and blotted her shiny forehead.

"I was going to tell all y'all about the cancer at some point. But, Lord, it's no real tragedy when a woman my age…"

"I want to know these things!" I shouted. Truth be told, my voice caught a little on the end.

Grandmamma's eyes went soft. She stepped closer, arms wide. I backed up, matching her pace step-by-step.

"I'm sorry I didn't tell y'all earlier. It's just, well, you know how your mother is. She'd rush home, drop everything…"

She paused. The silence thundered.

"…Lord knows all Candy ever wanted was to be a wife and mother. There's no way on earth I'd take that away from her, even for a second. Not after all that we've worked for…"

Grandmamma tried her luck by stepping forward again, palms up, in a sort of peace offering.

"…Plus, heck, I'm like a cockroach. Hard to kill," she said. As if that explained anything.

I stood my ground, my arms crossed tightly across my chest. She drew close and finally, I tolerated her embrace.

A single hot tear swept down my cheek.

Yes, I felt something after all, Maisie. And it didn't feel good.

"As for Natalya…"

The name stunned me back to the present situation and the twenty eyes gaping at us from across a platter of deviled eggs.

I shushed Grandmamma and pointed at our audience, before yanking her into the enormous walk-in pantry. I slammed the door shut. Through the slats, I could see the staff giving each other strange looks.

"You're not going to tell mom about the cancer?" I whispered.

Grandmamma shook her head, eyes cast downward.

"I can't tell her now. Not yet. The time ain't right. It just ain't right," she said.

"That's quite a burden to bear…" I thought out loud.

(And, Maisie, it's true: this news was a burden for a thirteen-year-old to carry alone. But you should know that the thought that I was going to use it as leverage—blackmail, really—against my Grandmamma did give me pause. A least for a moment.)

"So, no more lies, OK? I want to know the truth about Natalya. I think you owe me that at least," I whispered. "And, for the love of God, you can't tell my mom."

Grandmamma searched my face, her own lit into an eerie series of stripes by the light filtering in through the slats in the door.

Could I trust her? Would she tell Candy?

"Sugar, there ain't no way on earth I'd tell Candy about this sort of conversation. No way on earth."

Chapter 13

The Truth Can Hurt

Grandmamma set the terms: The following day, tea on the back porch, where she would sweeten the ugly truth with pralines and sugary iced beverages.

I rolled my shoulders, circled my neck in my room as two o'clock drew near, vowing to act as an adult or—more fearsome yet—a lady, no matter how terrible the tale. But, mostly, I vowed to pay attention.

Grandmamma wouldn't easily deceive me. Not again.

I arrived at precisely 2:01 p.m. Grandmamma was already seated in her wicker chair. Under her powder-blue merino sweater, her collar was starched and white as snow. Her face was still as stone but cast into a pleasant smile. She sat properly with her hands folded on her lap, never raising her voice above a ladylike decibel.

Maisie, Grandmamma meant business.

Pleasantries were exchanged. I was encouraged to sit. A glass of water offered (and declined). Then, a pause.

"Thing is, sugar, your biological mother, Natalya, is, a…Russian. A real-life Russian," Grandmamma began. She paused, apparently struggling to find the right words. "Now,

I know it might be hard to hear that you're not a full-blooded Acadian…"

"…I know that already, Grandmamma," I said, cool as sweet tea.

"Well, well. Alright then." Grandmamma took a sip from her tall glass. The ice clinked as she set the glass back down on the table. "Thirteen years ago, Natalya and your father had a little illicit affair, you see, because Walter's…your father's…"

Grandmamma turned her chin down, looked at me with her eyebrows raised, urging me to understand without having to utter the words aloud.

I tortured her with silence.

"…your dad's a spy, sugar. I know you know it already. And Natalya, being a Russian diplomat, well, he wasn't permitted to…liaise with her. The whole situation was terribly inconvenient. As these things often are…"

Grandmamma grabbed a praline from the delicate china platter in front of her. She nibbled.

Russian diplomat indeed.

I looked out, across the gardens and then, beyond, the vast back lawn of Black River. As with everything else on the estate, the grounds looked perfect. Any wild thing quickly trimmed, pulled, removed.

"But when Natalya fell pregnant with you, sugar, she made plans. She hid her growing tummy. Got ready to skedaddle, disappear. Made plans for a new life for you, her, Walter, wherever y'all could all live without…trouble. But…"

Grandmamma stood, walked over to the bar cart in the corner and poured herself a new glass—a short glass of something dark as amber. Before she turned back to me, I caught a flash of a dark look, like the kind that sweeps across one's face with sadness, anger, or regret.

"...but your father made a choice. And then all those plans to skedaddle got...thrown out. He left her, sugar. Left her knocked up and alone." Her lip curled up at the words.

I watched Grandmamma's eyes closely, willed her to look up and to the left, to fill in the gaps with unnecessary detail, to show me some, any, sign of deception. But Grandmamma's eyes remained locked and loaded. Straight as an arrow.

Natalya hadn't really been alone, not then. I was there, tucked up inside her belly. A Russian assassin's belly. Dad hadn't only left Natalya. He had abandoned me, like a box of mewing kittens in a dumpster.

"But things got even worse for Natalya, bless her heart. Shortly after you were born, a large man knocked on her door. Said she had been recalled to Moscow, immediately. Lord knows why. Perhaps Moscow had heard a whisper of the affair..."

Grandmamma took a seat back on her chair, swiveled toward me. Looked me right in the eyes.

"Natalya had one hour to pack her things and get on a black flight. Mr. Boris, with his six guns, would escort her there. Now, sugar, you gotta try to understand her dilemma before you pass judgement on her actions. Mr. Boris seemed to have no knowledge of your existence, a little newborn baby sleeping where you did best, in a bassinet in the closet. So, should she bring you with her to Moscow, where she was sure to be imprisoned—or worse? Or, let you go, possibly forever?"

Oh Maisie, you should know that I passed no judgement. I didn't understand—I couldn't understand—such a dilemma. After all, what, if anything, does a cold-hearted assassin feel?

Well. I suppose you know as little as I on the subject.

The cuckoo clock went off in the hallway inside, crackling through the silence, and startling me back to the present.

Grandmamma was staring at me as if waiting for something. But, yet again, all I felt was empty. Empty as a black hole. Grandmamma continued.

"You can guess the rest. Natalya packed her things. Slipped that precious necklace of yours under the closet door, along with instructions for the maid. Then she joined Mr. Boris in the kitchen, willing you to sleep just a few minutes longer. Casting her face into stone as she stepped out..."

"...how could you possibly know all this?" I had to interrupt. How on earth could Grandmamma lay out Natalya's dilemma in such detail just before she disappeared forever?

Grandmamma took another sip from her short glass—the one with the dark amber.

"Because Natalya showed up at my door three years later. Lord knows how she found me." She shifted in her seat, gazed out at the flock of geese that had just landed on the lawn. "She was looking for you, sugar."

For me.

For *me*.

The words echoed across the gardens, the vast spaces of Black River, Opelousas, my mind.

Well.

Was Natalya intent on assassinating me? No, that didn't seem plausible. Not when I had already disappeared. Not three years later.

Was it possible that she felt something for me?

Before I could contain it, smother it in rational thought, a warm feeling blossomed somewhere inside of me.

"Does my dad know?" I asked, quite evenly I must say.

Grandmamma took both my hands in hers, looked at me with her eyes squeezed in tight.

"Thing is, sugar, there is a whole other side of this story you gotta understand. When your dad suddenly showed up with you here in Opelousas, unwed, and tragically unprepared for parenthood, well, it caused ripples all across the county. Mimi, God bless her soul, made me promise to look after you as she left this life for the next, worried as she was for her only son and grandbaby. But, when your mom and dad started to get on, well, it just fit. You desperately needed a mother. And your mother, well, she was a little girl who had grown up clutching her baby dolls, smothering them with kisses each night…"

Grandmamma paused. I turned to see why. Her face glittered with the trails of tears.

"Sugar, you must understand that it was a cross to bear for so many years watching my own baby girl want a baby so bad knowing…well, knowing it would never happen."

I looked away respectfully while Grandmamma choked on her words, then pieced herself back together.

Manners are everything, according to Grandmamma.

I looked back when her sniffles had gone silent. Grandmamma had twisted her pearls around and around her right hand.

"So, Dad doesn't know Natalya came looking for me."

Grandmamma shook her head slowly. With her free hand, she dabbed her face with an embroidered napkin.

"Mom?"

Grandmamma sucked on her teeth.

Lord.

"And Natalya?"

Grandmamma paused, choosing her words with care.

"I'll always be thankful for what she did, Sugar. But you know your dad would lose his job if she came looking for y'all. Natalya said so herself that she was being watched, still, by the Russians. And, by that time, Lord, your mother loved you more than the very air itself…"

The praline crumbs turned sour in my mouth as the heading of this story became clear.

"…And?" The tone of my voice teetered on the edge of impolite.

"After three years in a Russian interrogation center, Natalya had found herself without means. So, we could help each other, you see! It was a perfect arrangement, actually. I'd help her with the money. And she could help you in the only way she could at that point…"

"…Which meant what precisely?" I shrieked.

"I told her that you were well. Showed her some pictures. Thanked her for what she did." Grandmamma took another bite of a praline. When a few crumbs fell to her lap, she brushed them off with the back of her hand, returning her pants to their pristine white. "Then, she agreed to let you go."

As if on cue, the flock of geese took off from the lawn in a cloud of white, passed over the single gnarled oak shading the back porch and disappeared over the top of Black River—to where was anyone's guess.

Chapter 14

Trust, but Verify

Maisie, why is it that obituaries are always about the nicest of people, people who spent their lives saving orphans and rescuing kittens? Where are the obituaries about the kind of people who, for example, stole babies, bribed mothers, provided funding to KGB assassins?

But I get it now. I do.

Because when faced with someone who isn't long for this earth, one tends to forgive. One tends to look at them in the softest light possible.

What I mean to say is that that day, as Grandmamma gracefully concluded her story by admitting to a felony, I didn't yell. I didn't call her names. I simply refused more pralines, explained I had a headache and gave Grandmamma one peck on each cheek.

Grandmamma has always preferred a continental goodbye.

I plodded inside, through the formal living room, up the imperial staircase and into my room, where I toppled onto the bed face-first.

A category 5 hurricane raged inside me.

Maisie, everything I thought I knew about everyone around me had been turned upside down in an instant.

I hadn't been rescued by my dad; I had been abandoned. And—worse—he had lied about it to me as we stood side by side in the desert.

And the one who had saved my life, ultimately, was Natalya—Natalya!—who had come back for me after all. For reasons yet unknown. For reasons I wouldn't allow myself to whisper aloud.

For the second time that day, something warm blazed inside, before I could douse it with the cold, hard facts: She was a spy. An assassin. And no one had seen her in a decade.

As for my beloved Grandmamma, well, what she did was wrong, Maisie, no matter how strongly she tried to cloak that wrong in right.

Oh, Maisie, I was sorely confused as I lay there face-down on my bed. A flurry of questions started to circulate, then suffocate.

What if my dad had lied about other things, too? What if Grandmamma was lying to me—again? Who, in these troubled times, could I trust?

Kiyoma!

My head snapped to the side and I caught a glimpse of the elephant necklace on my desk and my backpack slung over the desk chair. Deep inside the backpack, folded and stuffed inside my math workbook was Kiyoma's email address.

I sprung up, dug up the piece of paper and popped open my laptop.

I didn't know Kiyoma well, but unlike everyone else in my family, she had no reason to lie. And while she might not know everything, she could help verify some parts of Grandmamma's story.

My fingers danced over the keyboard as I considered what exactly to say. Maisie, I had to know whether I could believe Grandmamma. This was too important. Trust, but verify, as people like you say.

I settled on the following:

Dear Kiyoma,

Hey – random question when you have a sec. Do you think my mother loved me? This is important.

Sincerely,
Nora

As you can imagine, the magic of the Christmas season was a bit tarnished that year, what with me being surrounded by liars, spies and felons.

So, three days later, when my dad mentioned the possibility of driving into Opelousas to the cinema, I agreed at once. I needed a breather from Black River and all my delinquent relations.

Now, you should know that going to the movies in Opelousas is about as unremarkable as anywhere else on earth. But a strange thing happened while we were there— something that tipped me to the fact that this story was possibly bigger, even, than I had suspected.

(What I'm trying to say, Maisie, is that the plot thickened. Thickened like Grandmamma's darkest roux…)

We waited outside to buy tickets. I rubbed my hands together, willing them warm. I wasn't even paying attention,

I must admit. But something caught my eye nevertheless: out of a black SUV stepped a man with a crew cut, green polo shirt, pleated khaki pants, and loafers.

That man ain't from around here, I thought at once.

Now, that would have been interesting enough. But a second thought hit me and stuck like glue: I had seen him before. But where?

(Do you know?)

I was just about to point the man out to Dad when the man caught my gaze, did an about-face and disappeared around the corner.

I nearly forgot about him during our movie. After all, Opelousas is the tourist capital of the whole of St. Landry's Parish. Perhaps the man had escaped the big city life for a few days in charming Opelousas.

But three hours later, the man reappeared. In Jimmy John's Hardware Store.

We had made a quick stop on the way home to pick up three spare lightbulbs, a box of screws and a new door handle. I was walking a few steps behind Dad when I wheeled around, remembering that I had forgotten the screws in the next aisle.

But my eyes snagged on something out of place: the man with the green polo. Now he was investigating a shelf of nail guns like one would a crime scene.

Tourists don't buy nail guns.

I jabbed Dad's arm. But he was ahead of me, his gaze locked and loaded at the man in green.

There was no doubt in my mind: Someone was following us.

But why?

Dad, bless his heart, clasped one hand to my shoulder, tight, and wouldn't let go until we had checked out, exited the store, crossed the parking lot and clambered back into our purple rental Kia.

When we arrived home, Dad turned up the stereo in the kitchen and he and Candy spoke in hushed voices, their foreheads nearly touching.

I sprinted for the stairs, my heart thumping.

Maisie, I had a few guesses as to why Dad might be of interest to the CIA, the FBI, the KGB or—I don't know—organized crime. Dad would sort it out.

My interest was elsewhere: I hadn't checked my email in several hours.

After a quick scan of my inbox, I nearly closed the laptop. I halted mid-action. Hiding in plain sight in the un-bolded text of a read message, was a response from Kiyoma. My stomach did a pirouette as I clicked it open.

Dear Miss Nora,

I'm so pleased that you reached out.

To answer your question—yes, I am quite sure your mother loved you. I was so sure, in fact, that when you first arrived in my shop, I assumed that you were with Natalya. I think you will remember this was the case, no?

How did I come to this conclusion? Well, the day she came into my shop, she told me she had just purchased a farm and a little stone cottage on a hill in the English countryside—for you. She looked longingly through my elephants, trying to find the perfect gift for her baby girl.

To me, she was a woman who was already doting on her daughter.

But there's more, Nora. Last August, just a few days before you first came into my shop, I found an unmarked envelope slipped under the doorway. It was full of photos of you. It's how I recognized you at once.

Now, at the time I wasn't sure what Natalya was trying to tell me with all those photos. But now, I wonder if she was simply preparing me for your arrival. Making sure that we wouldn't miss one another. Making sure that I had a chance to tell you about that necklace and, perhaps, other things as well.

Either way, I hope you can see what I do in these photos.

Kind Regards,
Kiyoma

I scrolled down to scan through the grainy photos. In the first, a chubby baby girl sat in long grass looking up at a balloon, her eyes wide with wonder, her mouth wide with joy.

I couldn't suppress a smile.

The second photo was of me as a toddler, chasing bubbles across a grassy lawn, arms outstretched.

For the first time, I let the warmth inside me blossom into something real. Something that pulsed through me from the top of my head to the tips of my toes. Perhaps, just perhaps, Natalya had loved me once. Maybe still.

The third photo was of me wearing an apron but splattered from head to toe in paint. Preschool probably, I couldn't say for sure. Strange. I was older than I expected—perhaps four, or even five.

The fourth photo was of me sitting in class in third grade, looking at something off in the distance. I know I was in third grade because I only spent one magical year at the Hong Kong International School.

The warm feeling inside me twisted into something decidedly less pleasant. Something confusing. A bit eerie.

The fifth photo was of me playing soccer, running, cheeks flushed. Probably sixth grade, I couldn't say for sure. Where had these photos come from? How had they ended up under the door of Kiyoma's shop?

I lingered over the last photo, taken recently, just last summer, in Opelousas. I grinned with my innocent, pre-truth grin. But I wasn't looking at the camera. At least not the camera in question. I was looking towards Candy, Dad, Grandmamma, clearly visible in the foreground.

Was Natalya spying on…me?

Images flipped through my head: The man in the green polo stepping out of the SUV, a man who pulled out behind us on the way to school, a man in the souk, a man in the desert taking photos. E23257. E23257!

(Maisie, the subconscious is a powerful thing, processing an immense amount of data passively collected over months—years!—into something that is small, instinctive, and unmistakable…)

I blinked, clearing away all the dust. Natalya had a team—a team that's been trailing me for, quite possibly, years.

Chapter 15
Ask the Right Questions

Dad ran himself ragged during the next few days trying to draw out and identify his surveillants. Each day, while Candy, Grandmamma and I kept busy inside of Black River, he invented various errands and sightseeing excursions (The racetrack! The casino! The world-famous Opelousas museum!).

And each day when he returned—when he'd stomp through the kitchen cursing—a pang of guilt would course through me. Because I knew something that he didn't: Natalya was interested in me, not him. But, how on earth could I tell him that—at least without unravelling a tangled knot of lies?

He shook his head as he entered the kitchen after his third day without success. He turned up the radio in the kitchen. "Blasted idiots! Can't shake 'em loose. This just confounds me. And, Lord knows, I'm not usually confounded."

Candy gave him a nurturing rub on his back, as she always did, before preparing his post-operation refreshment.

I shot Grandmamma daggers with my eyes across the room. But the daggers bounced. As usual, she seemed blissfully unaware.

"Walter, has the thought ever occurred to you that y'all might be just a touch, what's the word...paranoid? Lord knows, there ain't been a foreigner in these parts for a decade, more or less," she said, shooting me a wink.

The pit in my stomach deepened. Since the previous day when I had scrolled through Natalya's photos, I teetered precariously between terror and joy over the fact that my assassin mother was hot on my tail.

Maisie, I know many girls have complicated relationships with their mothers, but this—the photos, the surveillance— brought complicated to a new level. Did Natalya love me? Did she want to kill me?

Lord.

"Naw, Aurelia. I saw it with my own two eyes. So did Nora. We ain't paranoid." Dad said, giving me a fatherly side-hug. "We just need a second sighting of the perpetrators 'fore I raise this up to the appropriate authorities."

What would happen to Dad—to all of us!—if the CIA discovered that Natalya was following us around?

You should know that I still seethed with anger whenever I thought of Dad abandoning both of us, then lying about it. But, still, I didn't wish for him to be fired. Not for the man who had made spying his life.

So dread washed over me several minutes later when we grabbed our coats and piled in the car, ready to drive into the historic city center for the annual lighting of the Le Vieux Village. If there ever was a time to draw out the surveillance, this was it.

Dad hummed Christmas carols the whole drive, never once swiveling to assess our surroundings. I glanced out the window a few times, cringing with the thought that someone had followed, that Dad would pick up on it. But I could find nothing out of the ordinary. Just the grey of winter dusk, and the colored lights of an Acadiana Christmas.

And several minutes in the black later, as we scrambled out of the car, a little flower of hope had blossomed that perhaps—just perhaps—I could enjoy this festive event without worrying about surveillance, spies, and assassins.

Tra la la la. What fun!

We strolled through the booths, made Christmas ornaments out of pinecones, took note of all the points of emergency egress. The usual. We sang along with high school choir singing carols. I even treated myself to a red and green cupcake as we waited, breathlessly, for the ceremonial "pulling of the switch".

Dad seemed jolly and gloriously distracted, gulping from his hot cider and puffing on his finest Cuban cigar.

I swiveled my head right and left with a warm smile of holiday cheer and the laser focus of surveillance detection.

Dashing through the snow…

I nearly choked on my frosting. My surveillant stood ten feet to my right, his hands stuffed into the pockets of his double-breasted peacoat (a peacoat, Maisie!).

…in a one-horse open sleigh…

I pulled myself together. I wouldn't be assassinated—not here among the crowds. I could find out a way to deal with that part later. The important thing, in this precise moment, was that Dad did not notice this man…

"…o'er the fields we go…" Dad bellowed to my left. He paused his singing, leaned down to whisper in my ear. "We're red, darling. Red hot."

…dashing all the way!

Jesus.

He hadn't even been looking, but, still, somehow, he knew. I turned to look at him. Stared in awe, really, as he took another long puff of his cigar, threw his arm around my shoulders and shook me with fatherly affection.

Truth is, Maisie, this was the very first time I considered what had heretofore seemed a ridiculous notion: was Dad actually a good spy? Would it dawn on him why we have surveillance now, and not during the previous three days?

Well. If it did, he showed no indication. Not that day. He simply turned back to the choir and kicked off with We Wish You a Merry Christmas, a particularly hearty rendition, it must be said.

We returned to Black River and I had made my decision: I had to tell Dad about Natalya trailing me. Else, he'd tell the CIA about the surveillance. Then, the CIA would discover it was Natalya, Dad would get fired and we would be destitute and homeless.

What I mean to say, Maisie, is that the stakes were high.

First, though, I had to warn Grandmamma about what I was about to do. There would be no convincing Dad unless I told him Grandmamma's secret—that Natalya had come looking for me. And, when I considered the range of Grandmamma's potential reactions, I feared for my life.

I stopped on the landing to still my beating heart. It was late. The night was black as velvet. The stars were out on full blast.

The thing about bouncing around the earth to huge, polluted capital cities, was that I never really saw the stars in my real life. When I was little, I used to think the stars here were all part of Black River's unique magic. Truth be told, they still made me pause in awe from time to time.

Night-time, after everyone was asleep, had always been my favorite time at Black River. During summer, I always stayed up late, propping open my window so I could hear the warm buzz of all the crickets and cicadas. Once, a few years ago, millions and millions of a special kind of cicada burrowed up from under the ground at once—rocking the whole county with their thunderous whirring, and blanketing Black River with a biblical shower of dead bugs.

Everyone hated those darn bugs and all their noise and mess. No one but me seemed to appreciate that their symphony was a natural phenomenon that only happened once every thirteen years. And, only here, on this precise spot on this huge, rotating earth.

Sadness washed over me as I realized that the next time those cicadas burrowed above the ground to sing, I'd be long gone from this place, my connection to Black River severed by what I was about to do.

I pressed my laptop against my chest as I pressed onward, tiptoeing down the hallway past Candy and Dad's room. I could hear their hushed voices behind their closed door. I didn't have much time. I silently descended the stairs and knocked lightly on Grandmamma's door. I heard a muffled voice on the other side and slowly pushed open the door.

Grandmamma sat in front of her bureau, applying her various night creams. I could see each vertebra of her spine through the back of her thin nightgown. When she caught sight of me in the reflection of her mirror, she turned quickly.

"Sugar?"

I almost flinched. Without her costuming, without her makeup, her dark eyes seemed sunken into her pale face.

For my whole life, Grandmamma had always been a force. Like those wild and gnarled oaks outside the window that bent, twisted, and, yet, somehow, survived hurricanes.

Now Grandmamma just looked, well, small. My resolve weakened just a smidge.

"Grandmamma, we have to talk. I don't think Natalya's holding up her side of the…agreement. I think she's following me. Been following me for years, actually."

Grandmamma's eyes softened into something that looked an awful lot like pity.

"Sugar, I know it must be hard to accept…"

"I have evidence!" I said.

But she coughed, interrupting. Perhaps she suffered from just a little cold, or a seasonal allergy, but it settled over the room like a bad omen, nonetheless.

"Oh, sugar. Your father is a bit crazy with all this surveillance stuff. I've been telling my girlfriends for years that working for the CIA has made the man nuts."

I popped open my laptop.

"It's not only the surveillance. Natalya has photos of me. Photos of me from as recently as this year."

I turned the laptop so it faced her, watched her face carefully as I scrolled down through Kiyoma's pictures. Natalya's pictures.

She didn't flinch. She didn't blink. If anything, she just settled further into herself. She looked extremely tired.

"Where'd you get these, sugar?" she asked, flat as a pancake.

"It doesn't matter! What matters is where she got them! She's been spying on me!" I was whispering, but high-pitched. "And I gotta tell my dad or else he's going to do something dumb and lose his job."

Grandmamma turned back to the mirror, regarded her reflection. The circles under her eyes looked like they had been carved out over years. Like the Grand Canyon.

"He's not going to lose his job, sugar. Natalya's not following you. Why on earth would she?"

Why on earth would she? What about the fact that she's a spy and assassin and has been blackmailed by this family to stay away from her only daughter? But all these explanations crumbled like sawdust in my mouth. There was nothing to say. Nothing I could say.

"I sent those photos to Natalya. And it certainly ain't a crime to send periodic updates to the mother of my only grandchild." Grandmamma picked up her antique hairbrush and worked it through her long hair. "I told you this was part of the agreement. I give her the relevant updates. Send her photos. There is no two-way street. She never responds, of course, except with a new address from time to time…"

I coughed.

"So you know where she is," I said, the reality hitting me like a bucket of cold water.

Grandmamma looked up at me, quickly, through the reflection in the mirror.

"And you lied about that, too," I pointed out.

"Oh, that's not true. Not at all. You never asked."

(Well, Maisie, she was right.)

Grandmamma placed the hairbrush back on her bureau, then turned it so it was lined up perfectly with the edge.

"So…where is my mother?"

"Your mother is in the room directly up the stairs."

"You know what I mean, Grandmamma."

She stood, walked across the room to her nightstand. Removed a little black book from the drawer. She flipped through the pages with her thumb. I could have sworn she was stalling.

"Sugar, I'm not inclined to keep this information from you. 'Course not. Wouldn't be right. But, I'd like you to consider what you're going do with it. Who you are going to hurt along the way. Your mom and dad…Natalya" She trailed off, then ripped the page out of the book. "What I mean to say is that little lie can be the kindest thing you give someone you love. Remember that."

She handed the page to me, then turned away as if she couldn't bear to watch me look at it.

Sieveringerstrasse 117

Vienna, Austria 1190

"This is where Natalya lives?" I asked senselessly, shocked by the ease of this discovery.

Vienna.

Grandmamma's back remained turned as if she were all of a sudden busy inspecting the white walls, the elegant look of her bedposts…

"Presently. She moves, often, so. Well, you decide what to do with it. Just make sure you think it through, sugar."

The paper shook as I folded it in half once, then twice, and slid it into my pocket.

I took one last look at Grandmamma's gaunt back as I quietly closed her bedroom door. I should have been ecstatic then, having discovered the specific location where my real mother lived, breathed and (hopefully) brushed her teeth. I had a lead—a real, verifiable lead!

But I couldn't shake a feeling that I had hurt someone already.

And, oh Maisie, it hurts to hurt someone you love.

Chapter 16

Master Your Poker Face

That left one teensy, tiny question: who was following me? Grandmamma didn't know that Natalya was a spy and assassin. She didn't know that she had all the skills to be able to track me across continents, over the years. That meant something. It had to.

But, truth be told, Natalya following me across continents, over years, did seem a bit, well, overprotective. Ridiculous, even.

Then, who?

Which led to another question—a slightly larger question regarding the slip of paper folded twice and stuffed into my pocket: What now?

Should I tell Dad that Natalya had come looking for me, as I had previously planned? Should I tell him that I knew where she was?

Impossible. That would end my search for Natalya—for good.

But what about the danger that Dad had predicted in the desert so many weeks ago? If he were telling the truth, I could be risking my life the closer I got to my real mother.

The image of the man in green haunted me every time I closed my eyes.

I unclasped my elephant necklace and placed it into one palm. Took note of the weight of the thing. The weight of the thing that had been stolen, hidden away in a closet and left behind. All for me.

No, I couldn't give up my search. Not yet. Not when I finally knew where to find what I was looking for. Not when I finally liked what I might find. If it wasn't Natalya trailing me, then Dad wouldn't be fired! And the surveillance? The danger?

Well, Maisie, I had this to say that day, buttressed as I was by my naivete: Danger be damned.

I barely remember the rest of our time in Opelousas. My mind was on overdrive with planning: how I could possibly get to Vienna alone, how to shake off my surveillance, what to say to Natalya when I found her.

And I ran myself ragged avoiding Grandmamma like one does a plague or a Yankee. Whenever she would step foot in a room, I would mumble and scuttle away to the farthest corner of Black River, only to have her reappear, smiling. The estate never felt so small before.

Maisie, it wasn't as if I believed that her cancer was contagious. Nor, if I am honest, was I particularly wracked with guilt over my attempts at elicitation, blackmail, and coercion.

What repelled me was that she reminded me of all that I had lost. All that I was about to lose. What I'm trying to say, Maisie, is that being around Grandmamma made me sad.

I do remember sitting at the foot of our ten-foot Virginia Pine on Christmas morning. I politely exclaimed over the gifts I unwrapped from Candy and Dad, respectively: a new hair tonic that claimed to straighten even the wildest hair (money-back guarantee) and a purple jump rope with tassels.

Just as I was about to follow them to the dining room table, lured by the smell of freshly fried beignets, Grandmamma pointed out a slim envelope still sitting under the tree.

"There's one more for you, sugar."

That day, she looked as rosy as a Georgia peach in her Christmas pantaloons. A pang of guilt tore through me.

I ripped open the envelope. Inside was a note.

Because you always loved it best of all, it said in Grandmamma's elegant cursive, *wanted you to know that it's yours. The lawyers said it is official.* Tucked behind it was a picture of Black River, an old polaroid faded by the years. There was a white smear in between the oaks lining the front-drive—the blur of a child in motion. Me, probably.

I looked up at Grandmamma, surprised. Her eyes had gone misty, but they dried quickly as she stood.

"Well, sugar, it's about time we tucked into something delicious and utterly damaging to our health," she said, standing. "Don't you think?"

"I'll be there in just a minute," I said, politely excusing myself. Truth be told, I needed a moment.

(Maisie, you know those moments when something happens, something that fills a need so deep and vast that over the years you lost sight of the size of the thing?

Well.

This was one of those.)

The next day, after collecting the last of my things, I stood on the gravel front drive ready to bid farewell to Grandmamma and Black River.

The breeze was gentle and soothing, rustling the leaves of the oaks around us. We all stood bathed in dappled sunshine. Dad and Candy were laughing about something as they loaded up the trunk.

None of it was right; none of it was appropriate to what we were really doing in that moment.

I grimaced, trying to keep the pain locked inside.

Grandmamma gave Dad and Candy tight hugs, then turned to embrace me.

Absolutely everything had changed between us, Maisie. And, still, somehow, her hug felt the same.

"See you later, sugar. Be good," she said, turning away rather quickly.

"Yep, see you later," I lied.

Then, thinking of Natalya, thinking of Grandmamma, thinking of you, Maisie, I prepared to cast my face into stone as I turned away from Black River.

Turns out, I'm lousy at that part.

Part Three
To Vienna

Chapter 17

There Is No Such Thing As A Coincidence

One day, nine time zones, and 18,016 miles later, we arrived back in Dubai. And remarkably, the next few weeks of winter passed without any international incident.

Dad reported our surveillance to his boss within hours of arriving and, thankfully—for reasons we didn't understand at the time—suffered from no ill consequences.

Bless his heart—Dad also began to stick to me like glue wherever I went. He dropped me off at school and picked me up. He lurked around the soccer fields during after-school practice, his hands stuffed into his pockets. On the day of our eighth-grade field trip, he followed our bus all the way to Old Dubai, careening around cars to stay within line of sight.

Al declared him 'helicopter parent of the year'.

I knew he suspected that I was the target of the surveillance. But, as a general rule, I asked no questions and avoided the topic. There was simply no way to move forward with my plans to find Natalya until I was clear of surveillance and Dad had assumed his normal level of parental neglect.

But, Maisie, you should know that he wasn't the only one paying attention. I, too, was on red alert during those first weeks back. I kept my head on a swivel, practiced memorizing faces and license plates. Took multiple modes of transportation to and from birthday parties.

But I never once saw my surveillant. I never glimpsed the E23257. And after three weeks of exhausting vigilance, both Dad and I seemed to conclude independently that we were in the black. Perhaps what we had seen was a fluke. Maybe, even, a coincidence (It seems so obvious now, though, doesn't it Maisie? That not seeing something can be just as suspect...).

Nevertheless, ever so slowly, life returned to normal. And, finally, I was free to brainstorm on how I could rendezvous with Natalya.

Now, I probably don't have to tell you that this would be no small feat, considering the circumstances. How on earth would I—a normal 13-year-old—travel from Dubai to Vienna, evade KGB surveillance and that of my CIA father, and find Natalya, a trained operative?

I'll admit, after applying the maximum brain power I had at my disposal, the only realistic idea I had was to send a letter.

That plan changed the first week of February. It was a Sunday. The morning sun shone sideways through the window of my homeroom classroom, blinding half of the class. I could see a terrifying amount of dust in all that brilliant light.

My homeroom teacher, Mr. Hardy, was marching up and down the aisles, blabbering on about something and handing out information packets for our eighth-grade trip. Many of the kids were chattering excitedly. My head was cradled in one palm.

Mr. Hardy turned down my aisle. The thick packet dropped onto my desk with a thump. I barely glanced at it until a single word caught my eye: Vienna.

I sat straight up. There were three options for that year's service-learning trip: Colombo, Nairobi, and Vienna.

Vienna!

I blinked, thinking it was a mirage. But the words were still there in front of me.

I felt a painful jab in the ribs, bringing me back to reality. It was Al. She leaned across the aisle so far that her chair tipped precariously onto two legs.

"A service trip to *Austria*? This school hasn't taken a single student to a civilized country with toilet paper since, well, since the beginning of time. This. Is. Awesome."

She tipped her chair back to level, landing with a dangerous clink.

I had to agree that it seemed almost too good to be true. Almost.

Nevertheless, several moments later, I carefully wrote a number one next to Austria, then circled the entire paragraph to emphasize my first preference.

I gripped the sides of my desk, willing myself to stay grounded despite the electricity racing through my veins.

Of course, Maisie, you know all about coincidence. Nothing is a coincidence. Nothing. Not for people like us. So, it probably doesn't come as much of a surprise to you that I found a note in my locker the following morning, just before the first period.

117

I cocked my head to the side.

For NORA, the envelope said.

Well.

Heat blossomed across my chest. Part of me was surprised by the note, Maisie, but another part of me had known, as soon as "Vienna" appeared on that paper my desk, that it was only a matter of time before something like this would surface.

(I wasn't such an idiot anymore.)

I looked left and right, confirmed that in the early morning chaos no one was watching. I ripped it open.

Dear Nora,

We need to meet tomorrow morning: 8:30 am, by Gate 5. This is important. It regards your mother (Natalya).

Don't be late.

V

A group of kids shouted nearby. One large boy nearly toppled me, bumping into my shoulder as he raced down the hallway. The tardy bell would soon ring.

Photos were clipped to the back of the note. I flipped the note aside so I could see them. All the photos were of me. Me with Dad walking from the front door of our villa toward our car. Me laughing with Al during our school field trip. Me sitting on the couch in our living room, my laptop propped open on my lap. Me sitting in the third period, looking bored.

The photos grew fuzzy. I made a move to rub my eyes, to clear the dust, only noticing as I drew my hand close how much it shook. Heat crawled from my chest up to my neck.

Maisie, if you've never seen a stack of surveillance photos of yourself, I can tell you that it feels strange. First, it takes the brain a moment to accept that in all these small moments, all these moments when your thoughts were blissfully elsewhere, that someone was watching. And then, something worse sinks in—something that could haunt you, possibly, forever. A question, really: Are they watching...now?

The bell rang. The hallway emptied of kids. Silence.

All that was left was me and the evidence that, despite all our vigilance, someone was watching. Someone who had been at home, here at school, in Opelousas. Someone who left the evidence as a lure, or, quite possibly, a threat.

And now, someone who wanted to meet.

Chapter 18

Weigh Risk Against Potential Gain

I stumbled through the next few periods. The babble of the kids around me, their playful screams in the sunshine, the school gardens bursting with pink bougainvillaea—it all seemed in dissonance with the question weighing me down.

What should I do now?

Third period. Art. From the second floor, I could see across the vast green athletic fields, over the school's high walls, to the desolate piles of sand just beyond.

Yes, I thought. Now there was reality if one dared to look.

I cringed as I looked up at each of the four corners of the rooms.

Was someone watching me...now?

I fought back a niggling feeling that I was, perhaps, a bit in over my head. Perhaps, a thirteen-year-old should not be left alone, pondering whether to meet a surveillant that had crossed two continents and counting...

I should tell Dad about the note. I knew that was what I was supposed to do. All his parental wisdom could help me navigate these murky waters.

After all, what if this were the Russian KGB, finally tipped off about my existence? What if they were here to assassinate me, to eliminate any trace of the illicit affair between their agent and the CIA thirteen years ago?

The threat of danger lurked in the dark corners of my mind.

But.

But.

Maisie, what if this was you?

It was a farfetched idea, surely. One that involved Natalya travelling the 3,505 miles from Vienna to Dubai, breaking into my school and slipping a note into my locker.

But it was possible, Maisie. And I just couldn't pass up a shot at possible.

Several minutes later, during lunch period, I chugged my chocolate milk and jabbed Al in the arm.

"I need to speak with you. In private," I whispered.

Intrigued, she dumped her half-eaten lunch into the bin and followed me outside. I made a figure-eight, on high-alert for cameras, surveillants. Finally, I selected a bench near one of the most lovely water features—the one that gurgled and sputtered (Brilliant sound-masking).

She slipped on her enormous white sunglasses and leaned back, letting the sunshine wash over her.

"What's this about, Curly?"

I pulled out the stack of photos and thrust them at her.

She sat back straight. I watched her face as she flipped through them. Her smirk evaporated and was replaced with something else, something that looked a little like confusion. Or fear. She lingered at the photo that included herself.

"What's going on here?" Her voice was soft.

And then I told her. Not everything, of course. I left out the part about the farm in England.

121

Her eyes were hidden behind her dark sunglasses while I detailed my predicament. She stayed uncharacteristically quiet throughout, until the very end…

"So, you really, really can't tell anyone any of this. But that's what's going on with me at the moment," I ended.

When the silence lingered, I turned to look at her. Her jaw hung open for a second, before turning upward into a smile.

"Curly, meeting you has been the best thing that has ever happened to me."

I stared at her, speechless. She kills me sometimes.

"Well. What are you going to do?" she asked at last. "About the meeting with your stalker."

I turned to stare out, across the throngs of elementary school children running across on the playground, the teachers chatting on the side-lines.

"I'm going to the meeting. I have to. But I need your help," I explained. "This could be dangerous. I don't really know."

She grimaced, stood up. "Then we've got some work to do, Curly. *Yallah, yallah.*"

She is the best friend I've ever had. By now, Maisie, you can see why.

For the second time that school year, we paced across Al's white-shag rug. This time, however, I did the talking. I taught Al how to pay attention, spot a lie, watch for surveillants. The basics. Then, I reviewed plan A and plan B and threw in a plan C for good measure.

"Who are you? No, seriously, Curly."

I shrugged (Because, naturally, Maisie, I had no idea).

Two hours later, our plan was ready. We would be in place at 8:25 a.m. The school would be quiet; the first period would have just begun. Al would stand at a distance, pretending to be on a phone call with her mother.

When my stalker arrived, she would look for my signal.

Yallah, yallah.

Chapter 19

Remain Flexible, for Things Almost Never Go as Planned

It was 8:25 a.m. and we stood outside on the hot pavement, just inside Gate 5. The middle school loomed behind me, the parking lot in front. Between us, the daunting security gate.

I popped my sunglasses on and looked left and right, front and behind. I wasn't sure whether to expect someone from outside or in.

At ten minutes past the tardy bell for the first period, the early morning chaos had evaporated. Now, there was only silence.

I didn't like this position, I realized. Too exposed. A chill raced down my spine.

Al gave me a quick nod.

I cracked my knuckles.

A white, unmarked van sped up and parked directly in front of us, on the other side of the gate. The windows were tinted, too dark to see who—or what—was inside.

The car's lights flashed once, then twice.

What did that mean?

I looked over at Al. She shrugged her shoulders at me.

I showed her my palm, urging her to have patience. Urging myself to have patience.

Current time: 8:29 a.m.

A man rushed through the gate, pulling along two children with untied shoes and untucked shirts. He didn't even glance at me. Current time: 8:31 a.m.

I scanned the parking lot, looking for someone, anyone.

"Nora."

Lord have mercy.

I swung around.

A man had walked up, silently, from behind. From inside the gates of the school. My eyes dropped from his stone-cold face to the visitor badge swinging from his neck.

I had never seen him from this close a distance before, but it was unmistakable: he was my surveillant. He was even wearing green.

(Of course, Masie, in retrospect, I realize that I was meant to recognize him. This was just another way of handing me a stack of surveillance photos. Oh, how long it takes some things to sink in…)

"First, your excused absence."

I was too stunned to speak but took it.

The slip had been signed by Headmaster Wooton.

"Follow me, please. Our ride is already here." He pointed at the white van in front of us.

I stalled. Something bothered me about stepping outside the gates of the school and into an unmarked, white van…

"Nora's not going anywhere unless I go with her. That's non-negotiable, *muchacho*," Al said. She was breathless from her sprint to my side.

The man paused, then—remarkably—nodded his approval.

"Noted. Fine."

Al and I followed him across the threshold of the gate. The security guard gave the man a wave (a wave!). And then the three of us climbed into the van.

Before we could even buckle up, the van peeled out of the parking lot and onto the highway. At blazing speed, we careened around the few other cars on the road.

"So, um, before you kill us, who are you?" I shouted. I grabbed the inside door handle to stop me from slamming into the glass of the window.

"I'm Valery. This is Roger," the woman driving shouted from the front. She was painfully thin, with pin-straight black hair and a black leather jacket. From where I was sitting in the back, her face looked set in a grim look of concentration. Or anger. I couldn't tell. "CIA Counterintelligence. We have a critical matter to discuss with you today, Nora. You too, Al."

Al?

I turned toward Al. She looked at me with wide eyes for a millisecond, then steeled them.

"How do we know you're who you say you are?" Al yelled back. She'd been studying up on spy movies, I could tell.

We exited the highway. The van careened around a roundabout, rumbled over the camel grates, then turned off the road. We roared up a dune and then stopped.

Valery unclicked her seat belt, ran her fingers through her greasy hair, then turned around in her seat to glare at us.

She first turned to Al, scanned her head to toe. Then, her gaze leapt to me. I made my face as blank as I could but still couldn't shake the feeling that she was X-raying me straight through.

Truth be told, Maisie, my heartbeat so fast I thought it might skip out of my chest. I'm pretty sure she couldn't tell.

At last, she plastered a ghastly smile onto her face.

"Great question, Al. I can tell already that you're going to be a great partner for us," Valery said, patting Al on her knee.

Al couldn't resist grinning back. Overachievers are glorified lap dogs.

Valery pulled a black wallet from her bag and flicked it open. Al and I leaned forward. Clear as day: It was a badge for the Central Intelligence Agency.

This was not good news.

"Nora, we are aware that you are undergoing an effort to recontact your birth mother, Natalya Petroviska," Valery said. Her CIA badge thwacked closed again.

Heat started to blossom on my neck. No, this was definitely not good news.

"Sweetie, you're not in trouble. This is wonderful, actually. Because we need your help. And you could use ours. We could be a team, you see," Valery continued. She paused to remove her jacket. Underneath, elephants covered her t-shirt from the nape of her neck to the edge of her sleeve.

Roger cleared his throat. "If I may, Valery. We're closing in on Natalya's current location. According to our analysis, she's somewhere in Vienna's 19th district. We are confident we'll narrow in on a precise address soon, and, when we do, we'll need your help in convincing her to talk to us."

Somewhere in Vienna? Natalya's precise location sat elegantly inscribed on a piece of paper, currently folded inside my math workbook. The thought that I was one step ahead of the CIA gave me a great sense of satisfaction, at least for a moment. But I suppressed the urge to broadcast that—yet. Because, even then, something about this didn't feel right. I couldn't yet put my finger on it, Maisie, but the feeling lingered...

"Why do you need to talk to her?" I asked nicely.

"Honey, let's back up," Valery said. "I have a present for you. Do you like this bag? Consider it a little gift between new friends."

Valery handed me a brown leather bag, embroidered with elephants.

(The CIA has a file on me, Maisie, and it says something about elephants.)

"No, thank you. I don't really like elephants," I lied.

A dark looked crossed Valery's face. Quickly, she wiped it off and tried on a different look.

"I see." Valery's brows became furrowed. Her mouth turned down, into something, I think, that was intended to look like concern. "Oh, Nora. We know your grandmother is sick. I'm sure that makes you sad. And why wouldn't it? Isn't it awful that you can't talk to your parents about it? Well, if you need someone to talk to, someone to help you process all that grief..."

A flash of anger swept through me like a white tornado. I knew exactly what this was and it smelled rancid.

I balled my hands into fists and leaned in towards Valery, so there could be no misunderstanding about what I was about to say:

"My Grandmamma ain't dead yet. You leave her out of this," I hissed.

Valery recoiled and smiled, I think, intimidated by my words. I tried the door handle, but Valery swung around to activate the child locks. When she turned back to face us, she had wiped the concern off her face. She resumed the grim look she wore while careening down the roads. The look suited her better, really.

I crossed my arms.

"Perhaps it would be best to just lay it out for you." Valery nodded at Roger.

Roger pulled a briefcase out from under his seat and clicked it open. With one finger, he slipped open a manilla folder labeled TOP SECRET and pulled out a stack of photos inside. He placed the first photo—an extremely unflattering shot of Natalya—on my lap.

I picked it up.

"Natalya Petroviska. Unclear if that's her real name or her *nom de guerre*, so to speak. Known to the KGB as Brass Leopard. Known to the CIA as Broken Arrow…"

"…Enough! Get to it," Valery interjected.

"Natalya is KGB's top assassin. Recruited when she was just 21 years old. Graduated top of her class. Now, part of their elite assassination squad, known to the KGB as 'Steel Door'. Known to the CIA as Opulent Rain…"

"Roger!"

Beads of sweat broke out on Roger's forehead.

He pulled the second photo from the stack and plopped it onto my lap. In it, a man stood smiling widely in front of the White House, standing beside a wife and two children, with another child—a baby, really—perched on his shoulders.

"This is Senator Jim White. From Kansas. Head of the Senate Select Committee for Intelligence. Lead author of a report due out next week regarding Russian hacking into polling stations all across America, right in time for the Presidential race. Our information suggests that Steel Door is in the process of planning 'Op Blue Lava'. We have moderate confidence, based on several first-hand sources, that Op Blue Lava involves…"

"…Nora," Valery interrupted. She put up one hand to silence Roger. Now it was Valery's turn to lean in so close that there was no misunderstanding what she was about to say. I could smell cigarettes on her breath.

"Natalya plans to assassinate this man."

No.

No.

No.

"Russia plans to control the outcome of the presidential race. The very basis of our democracy is under attack. Do you love America, Nora?"

I knew Valery was staring at me, imploring me to respond. But I couldn't peel my eyes away from the photograph of the Senator. The eyes of his children seared into mine, and my mind had filled with the incessant buzz of white noise. At some point, I became aware that Valery had started talking again.

"…we just need to talk to Natalya. Understand what her plans are. Protect this man and his family. Your school and headmaster are willing to do anything they could to help. I know you will, too. You can help us save American lives. You can help us protect our democracy. Not many kids get the privilege to serve their country in such a way."

"Do my parents know about this?" I asked, stunned.

I never thought I'd say this, Maisie, but I really could use Dad's advice at the moment.

Valery shook her head. "Walter—your father—has been compromised by his previous...romantic...relationship with Natalya. Plus, he would never agree to this. You know that. After all, he doesn't know you're looking for her, does he?"

I paused and cocked my head to the side.

Was that a threat?

Valery continued.

"Please understand that if you neglect to help us. With everything that we've already told you. With your biological connection to Natalya. We will have no choice but to remove you from the situation. Remove your father, too."

Yes, that was a threat.

I looked up sharply at Valery. She smirked unkindly.

"Remove?" I asked.

Valery nodded.

"Walter simply cannot work for the CIA if his daughter is in contact with a KGB assassin. How would we know if you tipped off Natalya? Or others? No, you and your family would be removed to a protective holding facility until we found the appropriate long-term solution. For your own protection, of course."

Al gasped and I jumped. Truth be told, I had forgotten she was sitting beside me. But during the last several minutes, she had turned pale as the dunes surrounding us.

"And would I also, you know, be protectively imprisoned?" she whispered. "Because, just so you know, I'm the lead of the middle school play next weekend..."

Valery smiled and patted her on the knee.

"No, no. You're fine, darling. We just need you to be a good girl and help Nora make the right choice."

Al exhaled and leaned back in her chair, relieved. Of course, she did.

Because Maisie—truly, what choice did I have?

Chapter 20

When in Doubt, Choose Action

To our chagrin, our excused absence slip said nothing about our meeting with the CIA.

"Meeting with the guidance counselor?" Al shouted as the van sped away from the curb, kicking up a cloud of dust and caking our uniforms with a fine layer of sand. "No one will ever believe this."

She was wrong; everyone believed it. And, as the day pressed onward, then the week, no one seemed to suspect anything was out of the ordinary. Certainly, no one suspected that we were working with the CIA to save a Kansas senator from certain death by assassination—at the hands of my real mom.

But over breakfast the next day, when I notified Dad and Candy that I had been selected to go to Austria for my service-learning trip, Dad slowly lowered his Gulf News so his glasses peered at me over the top.

"Austria?" he asked, his eyebrows pressed inward into a sharp V.

"Yes. Vienna," I said. I flicked my hair over my shoulder.

"And, pray tell, what kind of service will you kids be providing? Help with the ski patrol?"

He wasn't smiling, but I forced a little laugh. "Refugees, Dad. C'mon…"

Dad and Candy exchanged a glance I couldn't read—was it amusement, concern?—before resuming their normal morning activities. I planned to file away this interaction for further analysis, but it promptly got lost in the jumble.

Because Maisie, the weight of what the CIA had told me, the firm pat on the shoulder by Headmaster Wooton in the hallway afterwards, the terrible task ahead—well, it nearly crushed me during those dark weeks before our trip.

A warm feeling still blazed inside whenever I thought of all that you had done. How you had saved my life. How you had come back for me. But I wasn't yet sure: was that warm feeling love?

And, even so, could I love someone like Natalya? Someone who planned to choke the life out of another living, breathing human being? Someone who planned to choke out the very basis of America's sacred democracy?

Mark my words: it's one thing to dislike in the abstract the chosen profession of your mother. It's another thing altogether to stand by while she kills.

No, I couldn't do that.

(Can you blame me?)

Still. That gut feeling that first nagged at me in the CIA's unmarked van wouldn't go away. I knew, somehow—even then!—that something wasn't right.

So, Maisie: why didn't I tell someone? Speak up? Do something?

Well. I'll be honest: This wasn't really about Natalya at all. Nor Dad. Nor Grandmamma. This was about me. Perhaps it had been all along.

Because what hope was there for me now? I was the granddaughter of a blackmailing felon. I was the daughter of a cold-blooded assassin, and a lying, daughter-dumping spy. I was destined for darkness; I realized every time I looked in the mirror and traced the ever-deepening black circles under my eyes with my pointer finger.

Consider this as evidence, Maisie: Everything—everything!—I had done up to this point had only caused more trouble for all those around me. And, even now, I saw no plan of action that wouldn't bring even more destruction onto my family. Protective imprisonment. Interrogation. Destitution.

And all for what, Maisie—the truth?

The truth! Bah!

Truth was, I couldn't even trust myself to even tell right from wrong anymore. I was like a boat adrift on a glassy sea, with no rudder to guide me. No lighthouse, no compass, no heading at all.

So, all I can say in the way of defense is that the safest path ahead at that particular moment seemed to be wherever the winds pushed me, come what may.

I chose to do nothing, Maisie.

As promised, on Sunday, March twenty-fourth, twenty-four hours before our departure, an email from Valery appeared on top of my inbox. I stared at it for a moment. Then, I double-clicked it open.

Dear Nora,

As we are short on time, I'll get right to it.

On Friday evening, March 27, you and your class will arrive at Stefansdom Cathedral for a tour. I will retrieve you from there, and we will walk together to a well-known café. Our sources say Natalya has a meeting there at 6 p.m. She will be inside the café, meeting with another Russian agent.

I will wait outside while you enter the café. You will make yourself and your necklace visible to Natalya.

Do not approach her or attempt to speak with her, or you will be putting yourself in grave danger. I repeat, grave danger.

Once Natalya sees you, please exit the café. I will be across the street waiting, and you will follow me. We are confident Natalya will follow you. Together, we will lead her to a safe place where we can all have a little chat.

Leave the rest of it to us.
God bless America,
V.

P.S. Al has no need-to-know regarding the particulars of this operation. DO NOT TELL ANYONE.

Chapter 21

Never Wear Red During
an Operation

I didn't sleep a wink on the plane.

But the next morning—Tuesday—the sun still rose and set ablaze the cobblestoned streets and the elegant buildings of Old Vienna.

And when I first heard the clip-clip of the stylish Viennese bustling over the stones; when I first saw the coffee shops overflowing with people; when I first bit into an *Apfelstrudel*, dusted with the thinnest layer of powdered sugar, I just about broke out into song.

Lord. This place was fancy.

"Vienna is known for many things," our poor tour guide began that Tuesday morning. "Mozart, Schnitzel, our famous Lipizzaner stallions. But perhaps you are less aware of its reputation as 'spy capital of the world'…"

She paused to push her glasses higher on her nose as fifty jet-lagged 8th graders squirmed and whispered and, in one case, pressed a wet jolly rancher onto the back of another child's jacket until it became superglued.

"…By some estimates, there are thousands of spies here in Vienna today, involved in all sorts of illicit activities…" she continued.

Then the fog descended. Quite literally.

By afternoon, we shivered as we trudged through the streets in the mist and damp, between grey palaces and grey treasuries and grey museums.

On Wednesday, the gloom never lifted and, when night-time arrived, I couldn't shake the eerie feeling that the day had slipped through my fingers like a handful of sand.

By Thursday, I had gone mad.

I flinched when a man bumped into me outside the Hapsburg Palace. He mumbled a quick *entschúldigen*, then stumbled off, pulling his dark coat tight around his body. Did he pass a note?

I cringed when a woman with curly hair passed on the left, leaning close to whisper to her trench-coated companion. Did she say 'Nora'?

Well, did she?

By Friday, the stares of the little old ladies on the tram had turned sinister and accusatory. Were they KGB surveillants?

Under the glass chandeliers of Café Demel, snuggled up against the window, I carefully followed our tour guide's instructions to pair a half-spoonful of *Sachertorte* with a half-spoonful of fresh cream…

A man paused outside of the café—so close I could have reached through the window to touch him. He cocked his head to the side, removed his camera from his pocket, and then took a quick photograph—of the café, I think. Or me?

…the cake crumbled in my mouth and tasted of dust.

Why was everyone in this entire city wearing a suspicious black coat? And, blessed, where was the sun?

But Saturday morning, the sun finally broke through the fog. And then it stayed high and yellow all day—even throughout the evening as we walked down the Graben, past the ancient shops and the gorgeous golden statue of people dying from the plague.

The vast Stefansdom Cathedral loomed in front of us, daunting, dark and smoke-stained. Al and the rest of my classmates talked and laughed as we shuffled toward it. Pigeons cooed, then took off for the safety of the spires. A pulse of electricity raced through me from the tip of my toes to the ends of my curls, only growing in wattage as I neared my fate…

As if on cue, my arm was yanked down and sharply to the left and my body followed.

"Curly?"

Al's question seemed to echo across the growing spaces between us. Before I had even registered the change, I had been removed from the vast sea of tourists flowing toward Stefansplatz and the Cathedral—from my otherwise normal life as a thirteen-year-old. Now, I was on a different path altogether. I was walking side-by-side with a pin-thin woman in a leather jacket, white-blond wig and a very-unconvincing pregnant belly: Valery.

"Was I supposed to wear a disguise? No one mentioned that," I said, feeling flushed as we steamed ahead at titanic speed.

We turned sharply down a quiet alleyway. She paused, stooped down, untied then retied her shoe, looking right and left.

"Shhh!" she whispered. "Do you have the necklace?"

I pulled down the neck of my sweatshirt to display it hanging around my neck.

"Good. And you understand the plan?"

"Yes, I think so. I mean I hope so…" I shifted on my feet.

Valery stood up and scanned me head-to-toe. My face grew hot as I realized that my red, 'I'm in love with Dubai' sweatshirt might not have been the best choice for this particular situation.

She shrugged. "It's too late now, anyways."

Valery took off, shooting down a narrow alleyway. After only a few minutes, I was too out of breath to chat and she showed no interest in doing so. We wound through the streets in silence. I could have sworn we passed the same store twice.

At last, just as the sun dipped below the horizon turning the streets into bluish grey, we turned a corner and nearly crashed to a halt. An enormous building glowed ahead of us in the shape of V—like the bow of a ship.

"Here we are. Café Central."

A horse-drawn carriage clip-clopped by over the cobblestones in front of us, masking the pounding of my heart and hiding the café for a moment.

It reappeared. Chandeliers and gothic arches glowed from the inside, lighting up the whole street. A man pushed open the door, releasing the elegant sounds of a piano inside. The door clanged shut again as he skipped down the four steps. He was wearing a top hat. It wasn't a costume.

Valery's jab in the ribs yanked me back to reality. She nodded towards the café.

"So, um, Natalya's inside?" I asked (A delay tactic, Maisie—I admit).

"Yes, as we discussed." Valery closed her eyes and rubbed her temples with her pointer fingers.

Valery clearly has "stress management issues."

She opened her eyes.

"Our advance team has already spotted Natalya inside. She is sitting with a gentleman in black at a small, circular table. You will enter, then turn left towards the patisserie counter. You will find her there, between the *cremeschnitte* and the *strudel*. But you must hurry. She has already been inside for some time."

The what and the what? But Valery had already nudged me off the curb; there was no more time for delay. I took a deep breath as I climbed the four steps, then held it as I pushed open the door to the glowing café…

Inside, my senses were bombarded with elegance: the soft piano music, the gentle clink of silver cutlery on china, the refined, hushed voices of Europeans.

Naturally, I stood out like a sore thumb.

"*Entschuldigen, bitte.* May I help you?"

By the look on the doorman's face, he had said this at least once already.

"Oh, sorry. I just want to eat. *Pâtisseries. Yallah,*" I mumbled.

I spotted the gleaming counter of cakes and pastries to my left and shuffled towards it. Rows and rows of shiny desserts—red, custard-yellow, deep chocolate brown—lined the shelves front of me. I looked at nothing else as I moved toward them.

At last, I placed my palms on the cold glass of the *pâtisserie* counter and leaned forward to inspect the desserts. But, all the pretty, sugar-coated ladies just started to cackle.

141

My mind had gone blank! Was I supposed to look for the *schlosserbuben* and the *krapfen*? The *strudel* and the *kaiserschwarm*?

I flailed internally, shifting to Plan B.

My eyes jumped up, past the desserts, to scan the clientele beyond as casually as I could.

Miraculously, no one appeared to be watching me break into decidedly un-elegant face sweats. No, the room full of *kaisers* and *oligarchs*, assassins and spies carried on generally undisturbed by my presence there by the *mozarttorte*…

Except for one person, of course.

I recognized her immediately.

Just as my eyes swept past the piano, I found hers already locked into place.

Locked like they had been for an eternity.

Locked like it was inevitable.

Her ghastly face was blank and impenetrable, but her eyes were carved out by deep circles. Dark, wild curls danced gently around her face in what must have been a draft. But everything else about her remained as still as a stone—from her spiky black boots to her sharp, blood-red nails, to the tail of an olive-green dragon tattoo poking out from under her black leather jacket. Three cell phones and a tiny cup of coffee lay before her on the round table.

Well. She certainly wasn't PTA material. And she didn't seem particularly happy to see me, but…

She revealed nothing at that moment, really, except, perhaps, a slight cock of the head. An almost-imperceptible movement that I might have just imagined. A move which asked, without a single word: So, what now?

I had found Natalya.

And Natalya had found me.

So: What now?

Chapter 22

Trust Your Instincts

'Grave Danger' raced through my mind as I stood superglued to the floor, my eyes flicking between Natalya and the back of her extremely large companion, about thirty seconds past socially acceptable.

"*Bitte?*" The man behind the *patisserie* counter asked me, finally.

I took two steps backward, then swiveled towards the door. Willing my heart to be still and my legs to slow down, I marched toward it. The doorman looked at me with his eyebrows raised, but I pressed onward and he, with the exquisite manners one might expect of such an establishment, pushed open the door to hasten my exit.

Even though every muscle, every bone, every cell in my body implored me to turn around—to look, one last time—I resisted. Grave danger, I repeated thinking of the muscles bulging under her companion's faded black T-shirt. Grave Danger.

I stepped out of the door and out into the night. Then, when the door clanged shut behind me, I flew down the stairs and across the street, exhaling at last. Valery stood waiting.

"Is she…?" I started.

"…Don't worry. She'll follow."

Valery whipped around, and, once again, we were off at a clip. This time, a different direction from the way we had come.

Valery checked her watch, then took a sharp right.

We passed a man in a dark trench coat, his hand suspiciously hidden inside his coat. When I glanced back over my shoulder, I saw that he was following at a distance. So was another man I had not noticed before.

There was no sign of Natalya.

A U-Bahn sign glowed ahead of us and, to my surprise, we swept down the wide staircase into Schwedenplatz Station. Valery swiped two tickets and we hustled to the platform, bursting to the seams with rush-hour passengers.

In the anonymous bustle, I sneaked a look around.

Still, there was no sign of Natalya.

"Are you sure she's…?" I asked. I had to. Natalya had seemed so alien to me in the café, like another species entirely. I expected to feel that warm buzz inside when I first laid eyes on her, but, truth be told, all I felt was terrified.

"Shhh. She's here," Valery hissed. "Steady."

She's here?

The train arrived in a cloud of steam, and we jostled, pushed, really, onto a car along with throngs of passengers. As we pulled out of the station, I lunged for a handle, nearly toppling into a woman with an enormous fur coat. My nose tickled with the *mélange* of smells aboard. But I felt safe among all those people. Nothing could go wrong here.

Was I wrong to think so warmly of Natalya before? What if she had followed to assassinate me after all? A shiver ran down my spine thinking of the dragon tattoo snaking out from under her sleeve.

Without thinking, I drew closer to Valery, nearly leeching onto her back.

We pulled into station after station and, slowly, the train emptied. The streets outside the windows grew dark end empty. My fear grew.

Yet, we remained on board, even beyond the time when the back window was finally clear and I could see inside the car behind.

There, seated and calmly reading the Vienna Times, was Natalya.

The pointy toe of one of her studded boots wagged at me as the train jostled. My stomach dropped to my feet when I noticed a gun-sized bulge under her jacket. And in the car behind her, two men with dark trench coats—the very same men who had followed us from the café—glared at me with hooded eyes across two train cars.

We pulled into the last, dark station—Heiligenstadt—in a cloud of steam, the lights of the train flickering as we slowed to a stop.

Lord. What now?

"When we get off, I want you to lag behind me. Follow me, but at a distance," Valery whispered as we moved to the door, swatting me away as if I were a fly.

"But why?" I asked, trying to keep my voice steady.

"We want her to approach. Get close to you. We need you to do this, Nora. For America," she whispered as we stepped out onto the platform.

This was not part of the plan!

"But what about the grave danger…?"

Valery didn't respond. She shot off again, this time through the streets so dark that I could barely make out the back of her black leather jacket as she raced forward first to several feet ahead, then a bus-length and, finally, to a city block. Without the clop of her heels beside me, the city grew silent. Eerily silent.

I was alone, Maisie, surrounded by the CIA, the KGB and grave danger.

Anger at the universe took root inside my heart, then blossomed.

Why on earth would Valery leave me alone?

I glanced back over my shoulder. After taking her time to exit the train, Natalya had picked up her pace. She was now only a city block behind, her hands stuffed into the pockets of her jacket—or latched onto her gun?—I couldn't tell. She was within easy range to assassinate a thirteen-year-old in a bright red sweatshirt. I cringed, imagining the pain of a bullet tearing through my back.

What was she waiting for?

We took a left and pressed onward. I could now hear the click of Natalya's boots over the cobblestones behind me. Another glance back. I could make out her eyes. Her right hand was definitely latched onto the gun inside her jacket.

If she had wanted to kill me, she would have done it by now, I said to myself, trying to steady my racing heart.

We pressed onward, through a small empty park. Then, right around a café that glowed amber. I picked up speed to try to close the gap between myself and Valery, but she seemed intent on keeping me at a distance. The gap only widened.

Why was Natalya still following? She had to have seen Valery. Was she nuts?

I flinched. The dim streetlight illuminated a man as I passed—a man trying, unsuccessfully, to hide in the shadows. He grimly shook his head, as if warning about something up ahead.

Who the heck was he? And was that some sort of message?

I had no choice. I pressed onward.

Natalya's footsteps quickened as she passed the man in the shadows.

She was closing in. Why was she closing in?

My fists clenched as I plunged forward towards the unknown, the space ever widening between me and Valery and closing between me and Natalya. My anger at the universe narrowed into one, pin-thin woman with stress management issues. A pin-thin woman who had coerced me here, into danger, then—even worse—left me alone.

"Nora. Stop. Please," a voice called out from behind.

I slowed my pace.

Was the greater danger behind, or ahead?

Valery turned right and disappeared. This wasn't good. Even I knew that.

I walked to the point where she had turned: a narrow, dark alleyway with no visible exit. Natalya would never follow me in there; she'd have to be mad to follow me in there. But I had to see how this would play out; aborting now wasn't an option. I turned and tentatively moved in, slowing my speed even further.

Ahead, I could see a brick wall, and—possibly?—a left turn. But the dark played all sort of tricks on my terrified mind. It could be a dead end. A hopeless, dangerous dead-end.

Natalya's heels only clicked faster as she rounded the turn. She must have been jogging at this point...

Blessed. Natalya had followed me in.

She had followed me in!

What an idiot. A ridiculous, over-protective idiot.

I continued my march towards the brick wall and the possible left turn ahead, eager to escape the pitch-dark death trap. But, just as I reached it, twisting to see—yes!—there was light and a left turn ahead, I screeched to a stop.

And time slowed down.

Because, there, around the corner, were ten men with guns. And every gun was drawn and pointed toward me. No, toward the point where Natalya would, in just a few seconds, round the corner. And Valery stood in the center of that gang of armed thugs, arms crossed. With one bony hand lit to a ghastly white by a single, dim streetlight, she beckoned me to step forward, towards them. I could have sworn she was smiling.

That's when it dawned on me: this was no chat. This was a planned assassination. An assassination of the assassin.

I swung around to see that Natalya had stopped ten feet behind me. She could have no idea what lay ahead for her, but my pause must have given something away.

Even in the dark, I could see her arms swing onto her hips, her question without a word:

"So, what now?"

And, there, in that awful moment, staring at this strange woman across what seemed an impossibly large chasm, I realized I did have a choice. Really, I had had one all along, even though I didn't like it at all.

Because it wasn't Natalya standing in front of me.

It was you, Maisie.

It was you who faced Mr. Boris that terrible November day. It was you who slipped my necklace under the closet door and then left me alone, sleeping in the closet. It was you who made a terrible choice that day.

And I would, too.

I didn't understand everything going on. I didn't understand anything, not really. I might be hardwired for murder, deception, coercion. My actions might lead to protective imprisonment, interrogation, destitution. I ached, still, for the truth of it all—the truth of us, Maisie.

But I wouldn't be part of this.

Not *this*.

I shook my head slowly at first, then, as the sound of ten armed men shuffling toward me grew loud, I shouted at the top of my lungs:

"Run! Run, Mom, Run!"

I saw you hesitate, just for a moment, before you took off like the wind, your black jacket fluttering like a cape as you tore down the dark alley, past the two men following us, and—before a tear could fall from the corner of my eye to the tip of my chin—out of sight around the corner.

Chapter 23

Always Consult Your Allies Before Trying to Assassinate Someone

The ten men rushing at me from behind didn't worry me so much as the two—no, five—approaching from ahead, guns loaded and drawn.

Even though terror and adrenaline pulsed through my veins, I had registered one thing in the chaotic preceding seconds: you had run past the men in front of me and they hadn't tried to stop you.

They were not with Valery.

I swung back, then forward, counting more guns pointed at me than the years I had on this earth.

Lord. Where should I run? With whom was I safe? It didn't matter; I was surrounded. Like an already-dead pig in a blanket.

"Who the hell are you?" A man called out from behind me.

"Who the bloody hell are you?" A chubby man called out from the front.

I didn't answer; they weren't talking to me, Maisie.

"Don't you dare take a step forward or we'll blow you off the face of this earth," hissed Valery from behind.

"You think we only have five? We have twelve more on the way. Put down your weapons, blokes. Game over," said the chubby man.

A scuffle from the entry of the alleyway broke the tension, if only for a second. Fifteen guns turned together towards the ruckus. I squinted to see, but the dark was just too dark.

"Don't move closer. Sir, Ma'am. I implore you, don't move closer or we'll have to shoot…" the chubby man in front yelled.

The footsteps continued to race forward, without a break in their step. The men braced, ready to shoot.

I squeezed my eyes shut, preparing for what was inevitable…

"What the hell do y'all think you're doing?"

My eyes burst open. Candy broke through the circle of armed men, her hair frizzy and matted. If she was afraid of the fifteen guns threatening to shoot at her at any moment, she didn't show it. She swung around just before she reached me, her finger wagging wildly at each gun in front of her. I wouldn't have been surprised if she were foaming at the mouth; she looked so much like a madwoman. An awesome, frothing madwoman.

"Did y'all even notice there was a thirteen-year-old girl here? What kind of self-respecting person would point a gun at a child? At my daughter," she shouted. "Put. Those. Guns. Down."

Fifteen men looked at one another. Fifteen guns lowered, slowly.

Candy marched towards me then and gripped my arm so tight that I could have sworn she was trying to squeeze the blood right out of me.

"Yes, gentlemen. Ladies. I'd like to know what precisely is going on here," a voice rolled out low and slow.

Dad.

I strained my neck again as he stepped into the circle. Unlike Candy, he was as cool as a cucumber. He made a wide loop on the inside of the circle, looking into each man's eyes. As if he were stalking his prey. He was the only man without a gun, but you wouldn't know it.

"Who authorized this, this here operation?" Dad asked, spitting out the last word like it were bad milk.

Valery cleared her throat and crossed her arms.

"I did, Walter. These were my orders."

Dad continued his loop slowly—ever so slowly—until he stood directly in front of Valery.

"Ah, Tiny. I should have known," Dad said.

Tiny?

"You would have done the same if you were in my position. If you knew what I know," Valery said, stepping wide, as if to trying to make herself look larger.

Dad leaned forward and raised one finger so that it was inches from her face.

"No, Tiny. You see, I would never, ever put a child into danger."

"…Careful, Walter before you say something you regret." Valery took one hand and pushed down his finger. She turned slightly, so that she was facing her men.

"Something I regret, Tiny?" Dad looked calm, but something in the set of his jaw, the slight cock of his head, made me believe that, perhaps, he was not so calm at all...

"Yes, Walter. You know what people say," Valery said, but, strangely, not to Dad. Her words were directed right toward the ten men with guns. "What people whisper in the hallways at Langley. That you aren't quite the patriot you seem. That your liaison with Natalya may have left you...fond...of the KGB..."

Valery's voice went low, almost to a whisper, as she continued spewing venom.

"...that you might, just possibly, be working for the KGB from the inside, thwarting CIA's most sensitive operations. Funny, just like you and your daughter did just moments ago."

Valery nodded and ten men raised their guns again, this time, pointing them directly at Dad.

No, no, no.

"So I'd be careful about what you say. And, Walter, I'm requesting you to come with me. You too, Nora. So that we can discuss these matters further. At a secure location."

A vein on the side of Dad's forehead pulsed dangerously.

A few painful, silent seconds passed.

"So, Tiny, you're proposing to take me and my thirteen-year-old daughter into custody...based on a rumor? Last I heard, the CIA wasn't in the business of rumors. Last I heard, we dealt with facts," Dad said.

He turned ever so slightly, towards the men.

"Permit me, for a moment, to deal with what we know to be true. The facts, so to speak. You know what I find interesting? I find it interesting that KGB's top assassin has, actually, not assassinated anyone. Did y'all know you were about to put a hole in the head of someone who doesn't have a speck of blood on her hands?"

"You are not authorized to know anything about Natalya's file!"

"But even more fascinating to me is that the indisputable fact that there are five men here that aren't part of your team. Isn't that right, Tiny? Now, who might those men be, and why on earth would they be here with us now in this dark alleyway as we chat about these most sensitive matters?"

Dad turned his back to Valery and walked over to face at the five men who had trailed Natalya.

"Gentlemen. Your accent, your weapons, your finely tailored dinner coats. Let me see…British, right? By all means, not KGB or we'd all have holes in our heads already."

The chubby man in the middle took one step into the circle, then put his hand to his forehead, in a sort of salute.

"Yes, Sir. Mark Brown. Head of Countersurveillance, British SIS. That woman these men nearly shot is our top agent. The best and only penetration we have into the KGB. At great risk to herself, she's already thwarted fifteen planned KGB assassinations and counting. Our orders—direct from Her Majesty the Queen—are to protect her at all costs. All costs, Sir."

Mark Brown wagged his gun at Valery.

Dad nodded, apparently not at all surprised.

"I recruited her myself when she was only eighteen years old. Brilliant linguist. Nerves of bloody steel. Her real name's Maisie, by the way. From Wickenham. My mum feeds her cat, actually…"

Mark tried to continue, but Dad put up one hand.

"That'll be all for now, Mark."

155

He walked back to address the CIA men. "So let's be clear, not only were y'all about to put a hole in the head of a woman without a speck of blood on her hands, but also our best ally's best agent."

Ten men lowered their guns.

Dad stalked back over to where Valery stood and leaned forward, his face just inches from hers. Valery recoiled.

"Finally, I have to know one more thing. Why did it take a thirteen-year-old girl to loop me in on the fact that you were putting my daughter into danger? Putting her into danger, unnecessarily and without my consent?"

A thirteen-year-old girl?

Dad went for the jugular, leaning ever more forward.

"So, tell me, Tiny, shall we return to those rumors regarding my patriotism?"

A bit of spittle flew out of Dad's mouth and landed right on the tip of Valery's nose. I couldn't take my eyes off of it.

Valery took two steps back, making space between herself and Dad. Then she straightened her spine again.

"Walter, I understand your concern. And, look, I think it has been made quite clear that there are a few new questions regarding this case. But you are my subordinate, and this is neither the time nor the place…"

"…Oh, you have made it quite clear that this is a perfect time and place," Dad said, turning toward me at last. He glanced one last time over his shoulder at Valery, before pulling me into a tight embrace in the center of that strange, strange circle.

"Because, Tiny, I quit."

Chapter 24

A Good Lie Is Your Best Weapon

Approximately one hour and six minutes later, Dad, Candy and I stood in the middle of a dark and ancient square, gazing up at the Hofburg palace—that glowing monument to a complicated past. Dad had insisted. After all, we were in Vienna, and it was the very first thing we should see...

A single horse-drawn carriage rattled by. The streets smelled of roasted nuts. Glowing stone soldiers glared down at us from above. The silence was interrupted only by Dad attacking his cheese-stuffed-sausage-stuffed-bread.

Maisie, operations always work up a mighty appetite in this man.

I paused, inspecting my own *käsekrainer*. How anyone could eat at a time like this was beyond me. Plus, I couldn't avoid the topic any longer.

"Hey, so, Mom. Dad. Um, what are you doing here?" I asked.

Dad chuckled.

"Ah. A good question. But is it the right one?" He paused to take another enormous bite. A blob of ketchup squeezed out onto his mustache. "How are we here? Well, Al stopped by last week. Let us know what was going on. Said she was scared. 'Course she was, considering the circumstances. Unfortunately, we didn't know the particulars of the plan, except that this whole thing was some half-cocked counter-intel op. So we followed you girls to Vienna to investigate, and have been on standby, waiting for Al to tip us off that you had disappeared. Kicked off the operation, so to speak."

Al! Of course, Al would be too scared to keep her mouth shut. I clenched my fists, then released them as guilt and shame and gratitude and relief coursed through me all at once.

"The better question would be: to whom do you owe your life? That would be Al, my darling."

"But how did you know where to find me?" I asked, still incredulous.

Dad and Candy looked at one another. Dad waved his finger at his pork-stuffed mouth. Candy took the lead.

"Honey, we installed a little tracking device in your necklace awhile back. Just to be on the safe side. You're growing up into a beautiful young lady, after all, and…" Candy said.

A tracking device?

"…I have a tracking device?" I nearly yelled.

"Look, your dad went to great lengths to get the least invasive device. There's no video, no audio. All it does is transmit your precise location real-time to a mobile device…" Candy continued.

Was that supposed to make me feel better?

Dad finished chewing, then wiped his mouth with the back of his hand.

He smiled. He actually smiled.

"I installed that device years ago. You were only six years old. Now, if you think I wouldn't put to use the entire capability of the CIA to protect my little girl, well, you have no idea. And good thing, too, given your reticence to notify me of your involvement in an operation to assassinate your own mother. Lord, Nora. Some kids stick to sneaking out…"

"…I didn't know! C'mon, Dad, I had no idea that…"

Dad put up a hand to silence me. My head dropped, nearly hitting the cobblestones beneath us.

"But it must be said. You did me proud today, waving off Natalya, err Maisie, like that."

My head snapped up. What?

"To exercise that sort of sound operational judgment in a crisis situation. Well, I never thought I'd have a kid so, so…. you're simply a natural, Nora Jean."

Was that a tear?

Was that an actual tear?

The *käsekrainer* was tasty, and Lord knows Dad loves his pork…

Embarrassed nevertheless, I fingered my necklace. The necklace that had been stolen, left behind, blackmailed, implanted with a tracking device, and finally, used to lure a KGB assassin double agent into danger.

Lord.

This family loves in deeply strange ways, Maisie. That was the truth that washed over me there in the middle of Heldenplatz.

"What will happen to her now?" I asked. My voice came out small—smaller than I expected. Despite everything— maybe because of everything—strange was still something I needed.

"I've been thinking about that. She won't stay in Vienna. She's been compromised. She'll run and hide, that's for sure.

Until she's sure the KGB ain't aware of our little *kerfuffle*. She knows how to keep herself safe, I have no doubt. The question is…" Dad locked eyes with Candy. Without a single word exchanged, so many things seemed to be said. Candy melted into a hug with Dad. "Well, Lord knows you're not the only one who owes her an apology. The question is, how will we find her?"

Dad's face was darkened by the shadows, Maisie, but the way those shadows gathered under his eyes, the way his fingers danced across the back of Candy's black coat, already plotting, planning, surveying our surroundings, well, he spoke the truth.

"I know," I said after considering my words carefully. The answer, all of a sudden, glowed as bright as the Hofburg in front of us.

Dad and Candy released their embrace, looking at me in surprise.

"Opelousas," I said, nodding with the absolute conviction of a seasoned liar. "We'll find her there. I'm sure of it."

So that's my story, Maisie. And it's all true. Mostly anyways.

I apologize for going a little long here and there. For embellishing a bit for dramatic effort. But I hope you can understand that I needed you to see things the way I did. I needed you to see what YOU looked like to me.

It's true: I did terrible things for terrible reasons. But I did it all because I wanted to find you. I wanted to find you even when I thought you were a necklace-stealing, daughter-abandoning assassin of democracy.

And, even though you may never forgive me for putting you into danger, compromising your cover, leading you down that dark alleyway towards certain death, I know now that you once wanted to find me, too.

Well. Rest assured, I'll be looking for you. Soon. Right after I say goodbye to someone I love—someone who passed to me just yesterday one final, perfect gift: A few words and numbers scribbled on a scrap of paper so that I could say to my own mother, in just enough words:

I'm sorry.

Love,
Nora